KATIE IS TRYING TO BE FAIR—
AND SHE'S LOSING HER FRIENDS!

"Katie," wailed Jana. "How could you punish Keith and Randy? They're your friends."

"They admitted they did it," answered Katie, "and the court's punishment was fair."

"Was it?" Jana snapped. "Or were you just trying too hard to be *Her Honor*, Katie Shannon?"

Katie didn't know what to say. She had only wanted to be fair. She had to be, even if it was a friend who had been brought before the Teen Court.

"I've got to go now," Jana said. "I've got some things to do." She hung up, leaving the dial tone buzzing loudly in Katie's ear.

Katie sighed deeply and stood looking at the dead phone in her hand. So far, being a fair judge on the Teen Court was a lot harder than she'd thought it would be—because her friends weren't being fair to *her*!

Bantam Skylark Books by Betsy Haynes
Ask your bookseller for the books you have missed

THE AGAINST TAFFY SINCLAIR CLUB
TAFFY SINCLAIR STRIKES AGAIN
TAFFY SINCLAIR, QUEEN OF THE SOAPS
TAFFY SINCLAIR AND THE ROMANCE MACHINE
  DISASTER
BLACKMAILED BY TAFFY SINCLAIR
TAFFY SINCLAIR, BABY ASHLEY, AND ME
TAFFY SINCLAIR AND THE MELANIE MAKE-OVER
THE TRUTH ABOUT TAFFY SINCLAIR
THE GREAT MOM SWAP
THE GREAT BOYFRIEND TRAP

Books in The Fabulous Five Series
  #1 SEVENTH-GRADE RUMORS
  #2 THE TROUBLE WITH FLIRTING
  #3 THE POPULARITY TRAP
  #4 HER HONOR, KATIE SHANNON

THE FABULOUS FIVE

Her Honor,
Katie Shannon

BETSY HAYNES

A BANTAM SKYLARK BOOK®
TORONTO · NEW YORK · LONDON · SYDNEY · AUCKLAND

RL 5, 009–012

HER HONOR, KATIE SHANNON
A Bantam Skylark Book / January 1989

Skylark Books is a registered trademark of Bantam Books, a division of Bantam Doubleday Dell Publishing Group, Inc. Registered in U.S. Patent and Trademark Office and elsewhere.

ISBN 0-553-15640-3

Published simultaneously in the United States and Canada

Bantam Books are published by Bantam Books, a division of Bantam Double-day Dell Publishing Group, Inc. Its trademark, consisting of the words "Bantam Books" and the portrayal of a rooster, is Registered in U.S. Patent and Trademark Office and in other countries. Marca Registrada. Bantam Books, 666 Fifth Avenue, New York, New York 10103.

PRINTED IN THE UNITED STATES OF AMERICA

O   0 9 8 7 6 5 4 3 2 1

For Chris Schechner

CHAPTER

1

Katie Shannon felt like a criminal as she crept along the nearly deserted halls of Wakeman Junior High. She had hung around her locker until most of the kids had gone home for the day, and now she stopped outside the detention room and checked to the right and to the left, making sure that no one saw her.

"I've never had a detention before in my whole life," she mumbled to herself, "and I don't deserve one now!"

Sighing deeply, she entered the small room next to the principal's office where she had been sent to spend an entire half hour after school. This is disgusting, she thought, and *totally unfair.*

Four boys were already seated at desks, and there were no other girls in the room. Two of the boys she had only seen in the halls, and she didn't know their names. One was bulky and dark-haired, with the shadow of a mustache across his upper lip. He didn't look up when she walked into the room. Neither did the short, brown-haired boy with glasses. But Clarence Marshall and Joel Murphy from her old elementary school were there, and they gawked at her as if they were seeing a ghost. Joel pointed at her and put his hand over his mouth, while both of them doubled over with silent laughter.

Katie stuck out her chin indignantly. Those jerks! she thought, giving them both drop-dead looks. It didn't surprise her to see them serving detentions. Clarence and Joel had always been in trouble in Mark Twain Elementary.

She took a deep breath and marched straight up to the front of the room where Miss Wolfe, who taught girls' gym, was the teacher on duty.

"Miss Wolfe," she began as she handed in her pink detention slip. "I really shouldn't have gotten this detention. You see, what happened was—"

"Be seated, please," interrupted Miss Wolfe in her thick German accent. "And begin your homevork. If you have any questions about your detention, you may discuss them tomorrow vith the teacher who gave it to you."

Katie could hear Clarence snickering behind her.

"But Miss Wolfe," Katie insisted. "If you'd just let me explain."

"This is not the time to explain," Miss Wolfe said firmly. "Now, please take a seat and get on vith your homevork."

Katie clenched her fists and dropped into the first seat she could find. Her face was blazing from embarrassment. Her old classmates from Mark Twain would spread it all over school that she had been here. A lot of kids would laugh about it, too. Just because she never broke the rules and because she was always standing up for women's rights, a lot of kids didn't like her. Especially boys.

Not only that, this was the worst day in the world to get a detention. Tomorrow morning the teachers would announce the names of the three students from each grade who had been selected as members of the new Teen Court, and she wanted more than anything to be one of the seventh-graders chosen. Instead of sending kids to detention, Mr. Bell, the principal, wanted to try sending them to Teen Court, where students would listen to both sides and decide if the person was guilty. The Teen Court was also supposed to decide the appropriate punishment.

Katie lowered her eyes and pretended to be looking in her notebook for a clean sheet of paper. Getting this detention had probably blown her chances, she thought gloomily. And what made it worst of all was that the detention had been totally unfair.

Suddenly Miss Wolfe's shrill voice cut the air. "Tony Calcaterra! Vhere have you been? You know you vere supposed to be here as soon as school vas dismissed."

Katie glanced up at the boy standing in the doorway. He was awfully cute, with black hair and dark, flashing eyes and a small gold earring in his left ear. But as she looked at the way he was standing, so that no one could help but notice the muscles in his arms and shoulders, she groaned. This guy was a regular macho man!

"Sorry, Miss Wolfe," said Tony. "I guess I just forgot about detention."

"You didn't forget," scolded Miss Wolfe. "Not vith all the detentions you've had so far this year."

Tony Calcaterra smiled. "You're right about that," he bragged. "This is number eight, and school has just started."

Katie kept her eyes down for the rest of the half hour. For some reason she felt certain that if she looked up, Tony Calcaterra would be looking back, and she definitely didn't want to lock eyes with him.

When detention finally ended, Katie bolted from the room and raced toward Bumpers, the fast food restaurant where all the kids from junior high hung out. Hopefully her friends would still be there. Even though they all had totally different personalities, the members of their clique, The Fabulous Five, had been best friends forever, and they always stuck together. Christie Winchell was the brainy one. Beth Barry was the actress. Melanie Edwards was boy crazy. And Jana Morgan was their leader. Maybe one of them could think of some way to make her feel better.

"It's unfair," she insisted as she slid into their booth. "*Totally* unfair," she repeated.

"What happened?" asked Christie. "I heard that you got a detention, but I couldn't believe it."

"*Humpf.*" Katie made a face. "The detention belonged to Mona Vaughn and Matt Zeboski. You should have seen how they were acting up in English Lit class. It was disgusting. They were talking and laughing. *Flirting* is what they were actually doing, but did Miss Dickinson see *them*? Of course not."

"Then why did you get the detention instead of them?" asked Jana.

"It wasn't until I was warning them that they would get a detention if they didn't shut up," said Katie, "that Miss Dickinson turned around. Then she gave *me* the lousy detention! Do you have any idea how embarrassing it was to spend half an hour after school in the detention room with boys like Clarence Marshall and Joel Murphy? It was totally humiliating!"

Nobody said anything, and Katie could see that all four of her friends were trying hard not to laugh.

"It isn't funny," she grumbled, even though she knew that they really were sympathetic. "I didn't even get a chance to tell my side of the story. Miss Dickinson just wrote out the detention and that was that."

Beth shrugged. "She's the teacher, and teachers can do anything they want. They're in charge. They don't have to listen to anybody's side of the story if they don't want to."

Katie silently agreed.

"Teachers can't do just *anything* they want," argued Christie. "They have rules, too."

"Name one," Katie challenged. Just because Christie's mother was principal of the elementary school they had gone to, Christie wasn't an expert.

Christie bit her lower lip. "For one thing, a single teacher can't date another teacher in the same school."

"What about married teachers?" teased Beth. "Can they date anyone they want to?"

"You know what I mean, silly," insisted Christie.

"All I know is that I feel like an ex-con," groaned Katie. "And this detention will probably keep me from being picked for the Teen Court."

"I think you'll still make it," said Jana. "The teachers have probably already chosen the court. And anyway, which teachers besides Miss Dickinson and Miss Wolfe could possibly know about your detention?"

"I totally agree," said Melanie. "You're worrying about nothing." She grinned. "Were there any cute boys in the detention room?"

Katie looked at Melanie with surprise and hoped no one would notice the blush creeping across her face. "Of course not," she said quickly. "Just a bunch of animals."

She looked down and pretended to be totally engrossed in tearing the paper off her straw and forcing it through the tiny X in the lid of her soda cup. She could feel her friends' eyes on her as she took a long sip of Coke and tried to push Tony Calcaterra's face out of her mind.

Show-off! she thought as she remembered how he had swaggered into the detention room with a conceited smile on his face and bragged about all of his detentions. He acted as if he was such a big deal. He even sat there flexing his muscles as if he thought he were Hulk Hogan. She hated boys like that. So why was she thinking about him now? she wondered, and why had she blushed when Melanie asked about cute boys?

CHAPTER

"*H*ey, Katie! Is it true that you had to serve a detention after school yesterday?"

Katie stopped in the middle of the sidewalk and whirled around, shading her eyes from the morning sunlight. Richie Corrierro was leaning against a NO PARKING sign in front of the school and smirking at her. Next to him was Clarence Marshall, faking a look of innocence.

"What's it to you?" she snapped.

"Wow! Then it must be true. Katie Shannon had a detention," shouted Richie. "Call the networks! Get Brokaw on the phone. Get Rather! Eee-gad! Call Curtis Trowbridge! This is the biggest news of the year!"

Katie narrowed her eyes and glared at the two boys, who were doubled up with laughter. She hadn't been able to sleep last night because she was so worried that the detention would ruin her chances to be on Teen Court, and their teasing was the last thing she needed this morning. What was worse, a bunch of kids standing nearby had heard what Richie had said.

"What are they talking about, Katie?" asked Alexis Duvall, who was standing with Sara Sawyer. "You didn't really get a detention, did you?"

Katie pulled herself up to her full height, trying to muster all the dignity that she could. "It was a mistake!" she said loudly.

At that, Richie and Clarence began to howl with laughter.

"Of course it was a mistake," said Richie. "It's always a mistake when a *girl* gets a detention. Right, Katie?"

"You should have heard her," cried Clarence between laughing spasms. Then he raised his voice to a higher pitch in imitation of Katie's voice. "Miss Wolfe. I really shouldn't have gotten this detention. If you'd just let me explain."

Katie's face turned crimson as giggles raced through the crowd. She had never been so humiliated. Just because she stood up for the rights of girls, people such as Richie and Clarence never missed an opportunity to poke fun at her. That detention *was* a mistake, she wanted to shout. It was totally unfair!

"Hey, Marshall! Cut it out," called a voice from behind her. "How do you know it wasn't a mistake?"

She froze as she recognized the voice. It couldn't be, she thought. Not Tony Calcaterra. Why would he stand up for her? But when she glanced back over her shoulder, she saw that it was Tony, and he looked as cute today as he had yesterday. He was wearing a deep-red shirt that set off his olive skin and black hair. The earring sparkled in the sun. But he's still a jerk, she reminded herself, a macho jerk.

Tony sauntered past her. "You wouldn't know a mistake from a hole in the ground," he said, tapping Clarence on the chest.

Clarence braced his feet and stood his ground. "Sure I do. That earring's a mistake. I hate to see guys wearing earrings."

Everybody got quiet as a dark cloud passed over Tony's face. His eyes suddenly went cold.

"What did you say, Marshall?" he said in a low tone.

The two boys stood toe-to-toe, their noses nearly touching.

"Watch it!" said Richie. "Here come some teachers."

Katie watched as Mr. Neal and Miss Dickinson came out of the building together and walked toward them. The kids on the sidewalk scattered, leaving Tony and Clarence facing each other alone. Clarence gave Tony one last grimace, which Katie guessed was supposed to scare him, but Clarence looked more like a chimpanzee smiling.

As Katie walked on toward the school ground with Alexis and Sara, she was deep in thought. Tony's sticking up for her had seemed totally out of character. He had probably just wanted to show off in front of a crowd, she thought, and prove that he's a tough guy. Oh, well, at least the argument is over.

Alexis and Sara called good-bye and headed for their homerooms, and once she was alone Katie felt a catch in her throat. Her worst fears had come true. By the time the bell rings, everybody in junior high will know I had a detention, she thought. Probably all of the teachers know about it, too. I'll never make Teen Court now.

"And I would have been fair, too!" she mumbled as she walked along. "Really fair. I would have listened to both sides and done the right thing."

"Who are you talking to?" asked Melanie, rushing up from behind.

"Myself," confessed Katie. "I guess I'm so nervous about making Teen Court that I've started talking to myself."

When Katie slipped into her seat in homeroom, butterflies were dive-bombing in her stomach.

Mrs. Abernathy took forever to get her desk organized and call the class to attention. Finally she took attendance and then squinted at a mimeographed sheet in her hand. "Now for the morning announcements," she said.

Katie closed her eyes. This was it. In the next couple of minutes she would know her fate. She listened as

Mrs. Abernathy read with maddening slowness the list of activities taking place that day after school. Finally, the moment came.

"And now for the students selected by Mr. Bell and the teachers' committee to serve on the new Teen Court for the first semester," the teacher said. "Ninth grade: Kaci Davis, Kyle Zimmerman, and D. J. Doyle. Eighth grade: Shelly Bramlett, Daphne Alexandrou, and Garrett Boldt. And seventh grade . . ." Mrs. Abernathy paused and smiled at the class. "I'm sure this is the one you've all been waiting for."

Katie thought she would faint. Absolutely pass out and fall on the floor. Come on! she screamed inside her head. Get it over with!

"From the seventh grade," Mrs. Abernathy repeated, "Shane Arrington, Whitney Larkin, and Katie Shannon."

A cheer went up in the room, but Katie barely heard it. She was numb. "I made it," she whispered to herself. "I actually made it even though I got a detention."

"Katie," called Mrs. Abernathy. "Let me be the first to congratulate you."

Katie smiled weakly as the classroom erupted in applause, and everyone turned to look at her.

"Since you're the only member of our homeroom class to be chosen for this honor," Mrs. Abernathy went on, "I wonder if you would like to take this op-

portunity to tell us what you plan to do as a member of
Teen Court?" She motioned for Katie to stand.

As Katie slowly got to her feet, she realized with a
new feeling of panic that at least half of the class had
been on the sidewalk this morning before school when
Richie Corrierro and Clarence Marshall told the world
about her detention. They were probably thinking that
she was the last person in the world who should be
allowed to decide whether or not they should be
punished.

"Well . . . I . . ." she fumbled. The room had gotten quiet, and every eye was on her. What could she
say? How could she explain to them how she felt?

Katie cleared her throat and began speaking barely
above a whisper. "I'm very happy to be chosen for
Teen Court."

She was looking at the class, but in her imagination
she could see Richie and Clarence doubled over with
laughter and hear Clarence imitating her as she tried to
explain to Miss Wolfe how unfair her detention had
been.

I made it anyway, she thought with determination.
And I know better than anyone in this room just how
important Teen Court can be. Okay, she said to herself, sticking her chin out. Here goes!

"Now that I have served a detention myself," she
began in a loud, clear voice, "I understand some things

that I didn't realize before about getting into trouble. I know that just because you're a kid, that doesn't automatically make you wrong. Or just because it looks like you are doing something you shouldn't, that doesn't mean that there isn't another side to the story. So as a member of Teen Court I plan to listen to both sides and to be *fair*!"

The room was completely silent for a moment as if everyone was letting Katie's words sink in. Then the clapping started. It was followed by whistling and shouting and stamping until Mrs. Abernathy had to hold up her hand for quiet.

Katie felt a triumphant glow spread over her as she sat back down again. Maybe things will be okay after all, she thought.

CHAPTER

"*H*ow does it feel to be a judge?" asked Jana as The Fabulous Five gathered in the cafeteria for lunch.

Beth laughed as she pulled a sandwich out of her lunch bag. "Yeah. Are we supposed to call you 'Your Honor'?"

Everyone else laughed, too, except for Katie. "Actually being on Teen Court is a very big responsibility," she said, pointing a carrot stick at Beth. "Do you realize that when someone like Clarence Marshall gets into trouble, I'll be one of the people who will decide what to do?"

"Lucky you," said Christie sarcastically. Then she took a long drink of her chocolate milk and rolled her eyes toward the ceiling.

"Clarence isn't someone I'd love to spend a lot of time thinking about," agreed Melanie. "On the other hand," she added slyly, "look at all the time you'll get to spend with Shane Arrington and Garrett Boldt. *That* I could handle."

"And just think how much fun it would be if Laura McCall or Taffy Sinclair got sent to Teen Court," said Beth. She was rubbing her hands together in anticipation. "You could pay them back for all the nasty things they've done to us."

Katie couldn't help smiling at that. Laura McCall was the leader of The Fantastic Foursome, a clique made up of Laura, Tammy Lucero, Funny Hawthorne, and Melissa McConnell. They had been as popular at Riverfield Elementary as The Fabulous Five had been at Mark Twain Elementary. What was worse, they had set themselves up as The Fabulous Five's biggest rivals on the first day of school and had been causing trouble ever since. And, Taffy was their old enemy from Mark Twain Elementary. They had had a club against Taffy, and she had had one against them.

"What will you do if one of us gets into trouble?" asked Christie.

Katie blinked. "What do you mean?"

"You know. We're your best friends," Christie insisted. "After all, you got a detention, didn't you? What would you do if one of us had to go to Teen Court?"

"Good question," said Melanie, putting down her sandwich and facing Katie squarely. "What if it was unfair, like your detention?"

"That's easy," said Katie. "The court would listen to both sides. If the teacher had been unfair, you wouldn't be punished. That's all."

"Do you mean to say that you'd actually overrule a teacher?" asked Jana. "That sounds risky to me."

"Don't be silly," scoffed Katie. "This whole thing was the principal's idea. You don't think the teachers would have gone along with it in the first place if they weren't willing to accept the court's decisions, do you?"

"I don't know," said Christie, shaking her head. "I'd have to agree with Jana. It sounds risky. I'm glad you're going to have to figure it out and not me."

"I'll tell you more about it tomorrow," said Katie. "Mr. Bell has called the first meeting of the court for today after school in the media center. We'll get our instructions then."

When the bell rang, dismissing school for the day, Katie raced to her locker and grabbed her jacket and the books she needed for homework and fought her way through the crowded halls toward the media center.

She pushed open the glass doors and headed for the front of the room where Mrs. Brenner, the school guidance counselor, was directing the rearrangement of furniture for the court. Kaci Davis, who was in the ninth grade, was there already, as were Shane Arrington and Whitney Larkin from the seventh grade, Garrett Boldt from the eighth grade, and another boy Katie didn't know.

"Let's place these two long tables end-to-end and put the court's chairs behind them," said Mrs. Brenner. "I'll sit on one end, and the other faculty adviser will sit on the other." Katie put her books down and hurried to help.

"How do you want the other chairs, Mrs. Brenner?" asked Kaci.

"Put another table in front facing the court with two chairs behind it for the plaintiff and the defendant. Anyone who is waiting to be heard will sit in the room next to this one." Daphne Alexandrou, Shelly Bramlett, and another student came in and started helping. Katie was surprised when Miss Dickinson entered the room and started chatting with Mrs. Brenner.

"What's she doing here?" Katie whispered to Whitney Larkin, nodding toward Miss Dickinson.

Whitney looked at her over her glasses. "She's the other Teen Court adviser," Whitney answered.

Katie nearly fell out of the chair she had just sat down in. *Not Miss Dickinson!* She didn't know the meaning of the word "fair." Why, she hadn't even given Katie a chance to tell her side of the story about who had really been talking in English Lit. Well, maybe

Miss Dickinson would learn a thing or two from the Teen Court herself. Katie would show her what being fair really meant.

"Okay, let's get started." Mrs. Brenner checked the roll to see if everyone had arrived. As she called the names, Katie had a chance to look at the other judges. There was Shane, of course. Melanie thought he looked like River Phoenix, and Katie had to agree with her about that. Melanie would go out of her mind if she were ever in the same room with both Shane and Garrett Boldt at the same time. It hadn't been long ago when Melanie had gotten in trouble flirting with both of them and Scott Daly, all at the same time. Garrett was in the eighth grade and was sports photographer for the Wakeman yearbook, *The Wigwam*.

Kaci Davis was captain of the varsity cheerleaders and positively the most gorgeous girl at Wakeman as well as the most popular. The only thing about her that Katie didn't like was that she acted bored all the time. At that moment she had her little mirror out and was touching up her eyebrows as if they were on crooked.

Then there was Whitney Larkin. With her tiny frame and eyeglasses, Katie couldn't help but think that Whitney looked like someone who had skipped sixth grade and gone straight into junior high school, which was exactly what she had done. Whitney and Curtis Trowbridge, who was editor of the school paper, *The Smoke Signal*, and newly elected seventh-grade class president, were always holding hands in the hall-ways.

Daphne Alexandrou and Shelly Bramlett were both eighth-graders. Daphne, whose father owned a Greek deli near the school, was almost as pretty as Kaci, and Shelly was the star of the girls' basketball team.

The other two boys introduced themselves as Kyle Zimmerman and D. J. Doyle. They were both ninth-graders. Katie had seen them in the halls but didn't know them.

"All right, everyone. In about fifteen minutes we should have our first case, but let's talk about how we're going to run our court," Mrs. Brenner said, handing out pads of paper and pencils.

"Mr. Bell has asked Miss Dickinson and me to be your advisers. This is how it's going to work. Anyone who has had a complaint filed against him or her by a teacher or administrator that would normally result in a detention will come in with the person who filed the complaint. More serious offenses will be dealt with at a higher level. The person whom the complaint is against will be the defendant, and the person who filed the complaint is called the plaintiff. Both will sit at the table in front of us and tell their story. You should take notes and ask any questions you feel you need to in order to understand the problem thoroughly."

"Do we base our decisions on the rules that are in our student handbook?" asked Kaci, looking at her nails.

"Precisely," answered Mrs. Brenner. "There will be times, however, when the rule may not apply and the decision won't be clear. After we've heard the case, the plaintiff and the defendant will be asked to leave while we consider the evidence. We will discuss the rule that has been broken and how justice can be fairly applied when we are by ourselves. And of course, please remember that our discussions at that time and the way each member votes must remain strictly confidential."

Katie looked at Miss Dickinson, who had remained silent while Mrs. Brenner was talking. "Do we take it for granted that the student is guilty?" Katie asked in her most innocent voice.

Everyone, including Miss Dickinson, looked at her with interest.

"No, we don't assume guilt is automatic. Although, in most cases I think it will be more a question of degree rather than yes or no. You'll have some interesting questions to resolve in your own minds. Being a judge is not easy," answered Mrs. Brenner. "I'm sure it will all become much clearer as we hear cases. Miss Dickinson and I will be here to help you in any way we can.

"Now, we need to appoint a senior judge to control the proceedings, a bailiff who will lead the people in and out of the courtroom and advise them when we have reached a decision, and a clerk to keep track of the cases. Kaci, why don't you start off as senior judge; Kyle, you act as bailiff; and D. J., you may be the clerk. We'll trade off each meeting so everyone gets a chance to do all the jobs.

"If there are no more questions, we can hear the first case. Lots of luck, everyone."

Then, turning to Kyle, Mrs. Brenner added, "Kyle, here's a list of the cases for this afternoon. Will you bring in the plaintiff and defendant for the first one, please."

As Kyle left the room, Katie straightened up in her seat and took out her pencil. On the pad in front of her she wrote:

Case: _____

Defendant: _____

Plaintiff: _____

This was going to be fun. She would show Miss Dickinson how to be fair. If you listened to both sides, the answer would be obvious. She wondered why Miss Dickinson couldn't see that.

The door opened and Kyle led the French teacher, Mrs. Lemane, into the room. Behind her were two of Katie's good friends, Randy Kirwan and Keith Masterson.

CHAPTER

K atie couldn't believe her eyes as Kyle pulled a third chair up to the table, and Randy and Keith sat down. It was incredible. The very first case the Teen Court was going to hear involved the boyfriends of two of her best friends. Randy was Jana's boyfriend and Keith was Beth's, and they were never in trouble. She hadn't expected Randy or Keith *ever* to come before the court, let alone on the very first day. What in the world could they have done? It must have been the same as her detention, a mistake. Well, she thought, I'll just have to hear both sides and make the right decision. That's the only *fair* way. She cast a sideways glance at Miss Dickinson.

Kaci looked at D. J., who had the list of cases laid

out in front of him. "Would the clerk please read the complaint?" Kaci asked.

D. J. cleared his throat importantly. "Mrs. Lemane brings, against Randy Kirwan and Keith Masterson, the complaint of . . ." In midsentence D. J. threw his hand up over his mouth and covered up a laugh. He tried again. "Mrs. Lemane brings . . ." He turned away this time to hide his laughter. Randy and Keith shuffled nervously in their chairs and tried not to smile.

Both Mrs. Brenner and Miss Dickinson frowned at D. J.

Kaci reached out and took the paper. She glanced at it and raised her eyebrows before reading.

"Mrs. Lemane brings, against Randy Kirwan and Keith Masterson, the complaint of putting Alpo dog food in a casserole that was served to the seventh-grade French class." She shook her head and put the paper down as Shane turned his chair away. A smile was threatening to break out on his face, too.

Katie started counting by tens and gripped her hands tightly together to keep from laughing. The other students shuffled around in their chairs and stared up in the air, at the rows of bookshelves, or any-place else, to avoid looking at each other.

Kaci took her time before speaking again, and this time her voice was an octave higher. "Well, *hmmm*. I guess we had better start with you, Mrs. Lemane. Could you tell us more about the, uh . . . incident?"

"Yes," said Mrs. Lemane with a stern look. "It may seem funny on the surface, but the charges are *quite* serious. The class project was for everyone to prepare a French dish and bring it to class for the others to sample. Today Keith and Randy brought a dish they called *casserole au pois*. In reality it was Alpo dog food and peas with cheese melted on the top." She said it with a look of disgust on her face. "It sounded legitimate so I didn't question them, but one of the students suspected something was wrong and then others guessed its contents."

The judges on the Teen Court kept their heads down and stared at their pads.

"Randy and Keith," said Kaci finally. "Do you have anything that you want to say?"

Katie clenched her pencil tightly, prepared to write down that someone else had actually done it and that they were innocent victims. That had to be it. Randy and Keith were too nice ever to do something like that. What was it Jana always said about Randy? That he was kind and sensitive? Someone so kind and sensitive would never serve dog food to his French class. Besides, if the two of them *had* really done it, how could she sentence two kids she had known and liked from the third grade?

"We don't have any excuses," said Randy. "It just seemed funny at the time, and we did it. It was dumb, and we know it." Keith nodded his head in agreement, and the two of them sat quietly awaiting the court's decision.

"Well, uh. *Hmm*," stammered Kaci. She looked pleadingly at Mrs. Brenner.

"Are there any questions from anyone on the court?" the counselor asked.

Katie raised her hand slowly. "Did someone slip the Alpo in without your knowing it?" she asked hopefully.

Both boys shook their heads.

"Oh," was the only sound she could manage. Whitney, sitting next to her, made a couple of brief notes, and on her other side Shane was tapping the eraser of his pencil on the table absentmindedly.

Miss Dickinson broke the silence. "Perhaps the court should take time to deliberate now, Kaci."

Kaci jumped as if she had just been awakened. "Oh, yes. Would the bailiff please take the defendants and plaintiff into the other room while the court deliberates this, uh, complaint?"

When they were gone, Garrett spoke. "I'm in complete sympathy with Randy and Keith. It was funny, but do we have any alternatives except to punish them?"

"None," responded Miss Dickinson. Katie cringed as she continued. "They admit they did it. It could have been harmful to someone. Dog food is not meant for human consumption, you know. If you excuse them, someone else might do something worse, and how would you punish them if you let Randy and Keith off?"

"It seems a shame to punish them for something we all think was funny and that couldn't hurt anyone," said Shane.

"Especially when you think of all the gross things people eat anyway," added Whitney.

Katie thought as hard as she could. She didn't want to punish the boyfriends of two of her best friends, either. But they were guilty. They even said so. She would just have to do the fair thing. Straightening her back she pushed out her chin and said, "We all think it was funny, but it wasn't a good thing to do. What if someone had gotten sick?" She saw Miss Dickinson was watching her closely. "Therefore, the only *fair* thing we can do is give them a punishment that fits the crime."

"What do you suggest, Katie?" asked Mrs. Brenner.

"Uh . . . well. Why don't we have them help out in the cafeteria? You know, clean tables or something."

"That's not a bad idea," said D. J., looking at Katie approvingly.

The others nodded in agreement.

"For how long?" asked Kaci. Mrs. Brenner smiled as the students continued their conversation.

"How about for a week?" asked Whitney. Everyone agreed with her suggestion, and Kyle went to get Mrs. Lemane, Randy, and Keith.

Katie kept her eyes down while Kaci read the court's decision to her two friends. She felt bad about it, but it was a fair punishment. Wasn't that what the Teen Court was all about? She watched Randy and Keith as they left the room. They didn't seem angry or anything. She sank against her chair and breathed a sigh of relief. The first case was over, and how tough could the next one be? Every single one of her friends couldn't be in trouble. She giggled to herself as she imagined Jana, Melanie, Christie, and Beth all seated in front of the court with handcuffs and black-and-white-striped prisoner outfits on. Then she changed the mental image to Laura McCall, Tammy Lucero, Funny Hawthorne, and Melissa McConnell. Now that's a case I'd like to have, she thought.

Katie felt much calmer as Kyle went out to get the people for the next case. But when the door opened, and she saw who was there, she sat bolt upright. Walking toward her, with a broad grin on his face, was Tony Calcaterra.

CHAPTER

*K*atie strained to pull her eyes from Tony Calcaterra's. But they had locked with his, as if they were
connected by stiff taffy candy that refused to be pulled
apart. Finally she broke the contact and looked down
at the pad in front of her.

She frowned at the white, ruled paper. This is
ridiculous, she thought, shaking her head. It was embarrassing to be so confused by someone just because
he was cute. She had never imagined herself thinking twice about a guy who acted as macho as Tony
did. But she had to admit that there was something
interesting about the way Tony refused to be pushed
around.

"Would the clerk read the complaint?" asked Kaci.

D. J. gripped the paper with both hands and began, "The complaint of creating a disturbance in class has been brought against Tony Calcaterra by Mr. Naset."

"Mr. Naset, would you please tell us about it?" Kaci asked.

Katie peeked at Tony and quickly looked away. He was staring at her. And he still had that stupid earring in his ear. She had thought boys wearing earrings was against school rules.

"Tony was disrupting history class. It's as simple as that," said Mr. Naset angrily, sticking out his chin.

"What do you mean 'disrupting history class'?" asked Shane.

"You know. Talking. Trying to get the other students to laugh at him."

The judges made notes on their pads. "Did you ask Tony to quiet down?" continued Shane.

"I shouldn't have to. He knew he was in class. No one else had to be told to be quiet."

Suddenly Katie felt uneasy about the way Mr. Naset said it. "Did this happen at the beginning, middle, or end of the class, Mr. Naset?" she asked.

"What difference does that make? The beginning, I guess."

"Had the bell rung for the class to start?"

"I don't recall."

Something was nagging at Katie. She asked another question. "Was everyone else sitting down?"

"I think so."

Katie looked at him curiously. "Has Tony been in trouble in your class before?"

"Ha! Tony's in trouble all the time." Mr. Naset looked knowingly at Miss Dickinson and Mrs. Brenner, as if he was sure they would confirm what he said.

Out of the corner of her eye Katie could see a small smile creeping across Tony's face. He's so arrogant, she thought, why does he want to get himself in even more trouble? She leaned back in her chair, trying to decide whether or not to ask any more questions.

"But is he in trouble in *your* class, Mr. Naset?" asked Whitney.

"Yes. All the time."

"Tony"—Katie had to ask one more question— "why were you talking if the class had started?"

Tony folded his arms slowly and slumped against the back of his chair. "Like Mr. Naset says, I'm in trouble all the time."

Katie took a deep breath and pushed ahead, asking the question that had been nagging at her. *"Had the bell rung for the class to begin?"*

Tony raised his eyebrows at the force of her voice and hesitated a moment before he answered.

"No."

"No?" Katie saw the others leaning forward in their chairs.

"No. People were still coming into the room."

Kaci cleared her voice and looked at Mrs. Brenner as if to get reassurance before she spoke. "Mr. Naset, were people still coming into the room?"

"I suppose they were. One or two may have just come in."

"Were they seated?"

"Probably not. But that doesn't excuse Tony for making noise."

"How loud was he talking?" asked Shane. "Was he yelling?"

"He was loud enough to disturb the class."

"Was Tony seated?" asked Whitney.

"Yes," answered Mr. Naset curtly.

Finally the room was silent.

"Are there any more questions?" asked Kaci.

Even though Kaci was kind of stuck up, Katie liked the way she was taking charge. She understood why Mrs. Brenner had asked her to be senior judge to start off. No one had any more questions.

"Then, Kyle, er, bailiff, would you take them to the waiting room, please?" asked Kaci. "We'll have a decision shortly."

"I don't think it's fair," said Katie when Tony and Mr. Naset were gone. "When Tony got into trouble the bell hadn't rung, and Mr. Naset admits that the kids weren't all in their seats. I don't know how you can punish someone for talking if class hasn't begun. Who knows? He might have been telling someone else to quiet down." She glanced at Miss Dickinson as she said it.

"Knowing Tony, I doubt that," said Garrett, chuckling. "But it doesn't change things. If the class hadn't started, and Tony wasn't yelling or fighting, you can't say he was doing something wrong." The others murmured agreement.

Katie was dying to point out that it looked like a case of a teacher's picking on a student unfairly, but she forced herself to swallow the words. "Is this a case that we can dismiss?" she asked the counselor and the teacher.

Mrs. Brenner looked at Miss Dickinson.

"I think so," said Miss Dickinson. "It seems to be the *fair* thing to do." Katie could hardly suppress the smile that wanted to force its way to her lips.

When Mr. Naset and Tony were seated in front of the court again, Kaci announced the verdict. Mr. Naset's face tightened when he heard it.

Katie could feel Tony staring at her. Darn him, she thought. I wish he would quit doing that. It made her nervous. She was relieved when Mr. Naset and Tony finally walked out of the room.

Katie looked at Miss Dickinson. She had been fair even though it had meant overruling another teacher. Maybe she wasn't so bad after all. That just proved teachers could learn, too, she thought with satisfaction. Well, one thing was for sure. The cases couldn't get much tougher than the first two had been.

Katie picked up her things and followed the other judges out of the room.

"Don't forget we meet again next Friday," called Mrs. Brenner. "You all did a *great* job."

Katie pushed open the doors in front of the school and skipped down the steps. She was pleased with the way things had gone and couldn't wait to get home and call her friends and tell them about what had happened.

It was a shame that they had had to sentence Randy and Keith to clean up the cafeteria tables. But the boys had admitted they put the Alpo in the casserole, and the punishment was reasonable. Besides, it was funny. She was sure Jana and Beth would understand and laugh, too.

Just then she slid to a stop. Tony Calcaterra was standing by a tree, his arms crossed, smiling at her.

CHAPTER

*A*ll at once Katie's thoughts jumbled, and her face felt hot. She straightened her back and shoulders and surged forward, trying to walk past Tony as if she hadn't seen him.

"Hi." He fell in step beside her. "What's your rush?"

"I've got to get home." She gave him a quick, cold smile.

He walked next to her for a moment without saying anything. Her face felt as stiff as plaster.

"How come you went after Mr. Naset the way you did?"

"What do you mean, 'went after Mr. Naset'?"

"You know. You asked him all those questions: Had the class bell rung? and What were the other kids doing? Why did you ask him those things?"

"I wanted to know. I thought they might have something to do with the case."

"'The case'?" Out of the corner of her eyes she could see he was smiling again. She wished he wouldn't smile at her all the time. "I never thought of myself as a 'case,'" he said.

"Well, what I mean is, uh . . . you know. It's a Teen Court so everything we hear is a case."

"Aren't you worried that Mr. Naset might hold a grudge over what you did?"

"I wasn't the only one who asked questions," she said defensively. "Shane and Whitney and Kaci did, too." And then she blurted out, "Besides, it had nothing to do with *you*. We just wanted to be *fair*. That's what it's all about," she said, sticking her chin up defiantly.

"That's what I thought you'd say," he said and chuckled.

As they walked along in silence for a while, Katie was dying to ask him how he'd known what she would say, but she didn't say a word. She didn't want him to think there was a bond between them or anything.

"You have a boyfriend?" Tony asked suddenly.

Katie's arms tightened around her books. Then, trying to sound casual she said, "No, I'm between boyfriends." She cringed inside at her words. Boy! That sounded dumb.

"I mean, uh, I'm not dating." She felt the blood drain from her face. "I mean not anyone steady," she added hurriedly. Why don't I keep my dumb mouth shut, she thought angrily. She didn't want him to think she didn't date *at all*.

Tony said, "Me, neither." He was quiet for a moment and then asked, "Do you want to go out with me?"

She looked at him in disbelief. How could he think she wanted to go out with him? They were completely different.

"Not really," she said as coolly as she could.

"Whoa," said Tony. "The way you were sticking up for me in there, I thought you might be interested."

"Don't flatter yourself. The court was just trying to be fair," she answered stiffly.

"When you're interested, let me know. I gotta go." He took off at a trot. "Thanks anyway," he shouted back over his shoulder.

Katie stopped in her tracks. She was fuming. That *showoff*! How dare he think she was interested in him? There was nothing about him that she could like. All he wanted to do was fight and get into trouble.

Dumb! dumb! dumb! thought Katie as she walked down her street and turned into the driveway to her house. Why did she have to make a fool of herself in front of a macho guy like that? She had stuttered and acted as if she didn't know how to talk. How dare he think she wanted to go out with him? And she had *not* asked those questions at the Teen Court as a favor to him. She had just wanted to be fair.

She ran in the side door of the old white frame house where she lived with her mother and her cat, Libber. Libber was a scroungy-looking yellow cat that had staked out a claim on their back porch until they took her in. After they had taken her to the vet's to have her fixed, her mother said the cat was a liberated woman, so they named her Libber.

Katie's father had died when she was a baby, and her mother, Willie, earned her living as a freelance writer. Her real name was Wilma, but she hated it. Willie didn't make a lot of money, but like Jana's mother, she made enough for the two of them to live on.

Her mom was in the kitchen looking in the freezer when Katie came in.

"Hi, kiddo. How's it going?"

"Fine," answered Katie. "I made Teen Court."

Katie's mom gave her a quick hug. "That's great, honey. Congratulations."

Whenever she looked at her mother, Katie knew exactly what she was going to look like when she grew up. They had the same red hair and slim, wiry figure. She had hoped that she would develop at least a little more than her mother, but so far it didn't look like that would happen.

"Do you want chicken Parmesan or sole au gratin for dinner?" her mother asked.

"Chicken," answered Katie, plopping down in a chair at the kitchen table. Willie didn't have time to cook much so they ate a lot of TV dinners during the week.

"Mom," Katie said thoughtfully. "What if you knew somebody who was always in trouble and acted real macho, would you be friends with them?"

"*Umm* . . ." Her mother looked at her as she popped open a can of dinner rolls. "It would depend on how macho he acted and what kind of friend he wanted to be. If he didn't want to boss me around all the time or get me into trouble, it would be okay. But I'd have to like him. I wouldn't want to be pushed into anything. Is someone trying to push you around, honey?"

"Kind of." Katie knew her mother wouldn't be pushed into anything. She was tough, and Katie wanted to be just like her. She had even tried to get her friends in The Fabulous Five to be more liberated. When Christie was running for seventh-grade class president, Katie had wanted her to put a feminist plank in her platform, but her friends had vetoed the idea.

Libber wrapped herself around Katie's leg, and Katie reached down to stroke her as her thoughts went back to Tony Calcaterra. He was exactly the kind of macho boyfriend she did *not* want to have. It was revolting the way he strutted around showing off his arms. She wanted a boy who would appreciate her as an equal. She bet he even watched wrestling on TV all the time.

After dinner, her mother went back to her office to work on an article for a magazine, and Katie decided to call her friends and tell them about the Teen Court. She knew they would be as excited as she was. She dialed Jana's number first.

"Hi." Jana's voice sounded chirpy as usual. "How did the court go?"

"Great. We had two cases, but I hate to tell you that Randy Kirwan and Keith Masterson were in the very first one. You won't believe what they did," she said, laughing. "It *was* kind of funny, but it was a bad thing to do. They made a casserole out of Alpo dog food and peas covered with melted cheese for French class, and some of the kids and teachers actually ate some of it."

The telephone line was silent for a moment, and then Jana asked, "What did the court do?"

"What could we do? Randy and Keith both admitted they did it and said it was a dumb thing to do. We sentenced them to clean the tables in the cafeteria after lunch for the next week."

"Katie," wailed Jana. "How could you punish your friends? It was just a joke."

"But people *ate* it."

"People probably eat things that are a lot worse. Why didn't you stick up for them?"

"They admitted they did it," answered Katie, "and the punishment was fair."

"Was it? Or were you just trying too hard to be *Her Honor*, Katie Shannon?"

Katie didn't know what to say. She had only wanted to be fair. She had to be, even if it was a friend who had been brought before the Teen Court.

"I've got to go now," Jana said. "I've got some things to do." She hung up, leaving the dial tone buzzing loudly in Katie's ear.

Katie sighed deeply and stood looking at the dead phone in her hand.

CHAPTER

7

Katie put the receiver in its cradle and tried to figure out what had just happened. How could Jana be mad at her? She had only done what was right. The other judges would have thought that she was just trying to protect her friends if she had argued against punishing Randy and Keith. Shane and Whitney had talked about not punishing them, but Miss Dickinson and Mrs. Brenner had said the court had to. Randy and Keith had even said themselves that what they had done was dumb.

She hesitated. Should she call Beth? Beth would probably be mad at her, too, when she found out about Randy and Keith. Well, she might as well get it over with.

Katie had been right. Beth didn't like it any more than Jana had.

"YOU WHAT?!" shrieked Beth. "How could you do such a thing? I mean, they're your friends."

"It wasn't just me," Katie defended herself as well as she could. "I'm not the only one on the Teen Court, you know."

"But it will be on their records, like criminals. It could follow them through life—keep them from getting into college or getting a job."

"Don't be so melodramatic," answered Katie. "It's not as if they're going to lose their citizenship over it. They'll survive. They admitted that they shouldn't have done it."

"What if they had done something really bad? Would you have hung them?"

Beth was going too far. "Now wait a minute," interrupted Katie. "I couldn't argue that they shouldn't be punished just because they're my friends."

"*Ex*-friends, probably."

"Come on, Beth. The court has to be *fair*."

"Well, I don't think that it was."

Katie sighed after they hung up. Boy, were Beth and Jana being unreasonable.

She wandered into Willie's office. Her mother's office was in the tiny bedroom at the front of the house. The desk and the small table next to it were always cluttered with piles of papers where Libber made a nest to lie in the sun while Willie was working. It always comforted Katie to see her mother tapping on the keys and staring at the big blue eye of her secondhand computer as she was now. Somehow it seemed that everything would be okay.

"Mom."

"Yes, sweetheart?" Willie made a note on a pad beside her keyboard and glanced at Katie. "What's up?"

"Oh, nothing."

Katie fingered through some papers on the table.

Willie put her pencil down. " 'Nothing' can be quite a bit sometimes. Want to tell me about it?"

Katie sat down on the edge of the table. "I was just thinking about how hard it is to know what's fair sometimes. You always seem to know what's right. Sometimes I know, and sometimes I don't."

Her mother leaned back and looked at her thoughtfully. "I'm glad you think I do. The truth is, I don't always know."

"How do you know when you're maybe being too tough on someone?"

Willie shrugged. "Sometimes you just have to trust your own judgment. If you feel inside of you that something is right, you should go with it. Most of the time you'll be right. If you aren't, well, you know you did your best, and you'll probably learn something from it."

Katie sighed. Why did things always sound easier than they really were?

For the rest of the weekend, Katie tried not to think too much about the Teen Court. On Sunday morning an article in the newspaper caught her eye. "It's about Teen Court, and there's even a picture of Mr. Bell with it," Katie cried excitedly as she pointed it out to her mother.

"Terrific. Let's see what it says," said Willie. Katie sat down on the sofa beside her, and they read it together.

Wakeman Junior High Appoints Experimental Teen Court

William Bell, principal of Wakeman Junior High, announced today the appointment of nine students and two teachers to an experimental Teen Court in the hopes of doing away with the detention system. Bell said that he thought the experiment would be a useful lesson for students in how the judicial system works. He also expressed the hope that peers sitting in judgment of each other would reduce the volume of student rule infractions.

Student jurors are: seventh-graders, Whitney Larkin, Shane Arrington, Katie Shannon; eighth-graders, Daphne Alexandrou, Shelly Bramlett,

*Garrett Boldt; and ninth-graders, Kaci Davis,
Kyle Zimmerman, D. J. Doyle. Teachers are Mrs.
Joyce Brenner, school guidance counselor, and Miss
Elizabeth Dickinson, English teacher.*
    Teen Court heard its first cases on Friday.

"Hey, we're famous," said Katie. "Everybody in
town will know about us now."

When Katie got to school on Monday morning, lots of
kids were talking about the article, and several called
out to her.

"Hey, Katie," shouted Alexis. "I saw your name in
the paper yesterday. Way to go!"

Her friends were waiting at their special place by the
fence. They all said "Hi," but Jana and Beth didn't
smile the way they usually did.

"That was a neat article in the paper about Teen
Court," said Christie. "How did the first session go?"

Katie cringed. Why did she have to ask that in front
of Jana and Beth? "Okay." Then to change the subject
she quickly asked, "Did you and Jon play tennis this
weekend?"

Christie nodded. "Sure did, and my backhand is
getting better now that I don't have somebody looking
over my shoulder all the time." Katie knew she was
referring to the way her father had always pressured
her to play competition tennis. He had lined up one

instructor after another until Christie had finally told her parents that she only wanted to play tennis for fun.

"What are Jon's mom and dad really like?" asked Melanie, who somehow always managed to bring the conversation around to subjects that had to do with boyfriends. Jon's father, Chip Smith, was a television sports director, and his mother, Marge Whitworth, was a TV news anchor with her own talk show. "Do they have big shiny perfect teeth the way they look on TV?"

"Kind of," admitted Christie. "They're both a little hyper. Jon isn't at all like them."

"I still haven't gotten over the way you and Jon came up with that idea for a mystery candidate for seventh-grade class president," said Jana, shaking her head and smiling. "That had all of Wacko Junior High guessing."

"Yeah," said Melanie. "And Laura McCall was furious when Melissa McConnell didn't win."

"Speaking of Laura," broke in Beth, "here she comes with her little ducklings right behind her." Laura McCall was headed toward The Fabulous Five, and right behind her were Melissa McConnell, Tammy Lucero and Funny Hawthorne.

"Well, if it isn't the supreme court justice and her friends," said Laura, speaking directly to Katie.

Beth stepped in between Katie and Laura. "Well, at least you're admitting there's something supreme about us, which is more than we can say about you."

It made Katie feel good when she realized that her friend was trying to protect her even though Beth was still a little angry over Keith and Randy's being punished.

Laura switched her long braid back and forth with one hand like a cat switching its tail. "I understand Teen Court made some big decisions last Friday. Like making Randy Kirwan and Keith Masterson clean tables in the cafeteria. I suppose that was your idea. Now is that any way to treat friends?"

Katie felt Jana and Beth recoil from the words, and a knot came into her stomach. Laura had heard about the punishment and wanted to make sure that Jana and Beth were mad at her. If she only knew how mad they were already, Katie knew she would be overjoyed.

Christie jumped to her defense. "You wouldn't know about making important decisions like the Teen Court does. All you worry about is how to have parties and make your friends do what you want them to do."

Katie saw Christie had hit a tender spot. Laura's eyes narrowed and they seemed to spit fire.

"Well," she said slowly, "if punishing your friends' boyfriends and letting your own boyfriend off is an important decision, I guess I don't."

"What do you mean?" asked Jana, her eyes narrowing.

"Oh, didn't you know?" Laura was smiling sweetly and swinging her braid slowly. Katie knew she didn't want to hear what she was going to say next.

"It's easy to figure out that Katie was the one who talked the Teen Court into letting Tony Calcaterra off after he caused a near riot in class. We saw them walking home together after school on Friday."

Katie was miserable in the silence that followed Laura's words. This time none of The Fabulous Five spoke up.

CHAPTER

*A*s Laura McCall and the others drifted off, Katie's friends turned and glared at her. "You argued for letting Tony Calcaterra off?" asked Beth. "You know he's in trouble all the time. Randy and Keith are never in trouble. Why didn't you argue for them?"

"Wait a minute," said Katie, putting up her hands to fend Beth off. "She doesn't know what she's talking about. I didn't argue *for* anybody. I just asked questions about what was going on in the classroom when Tony was supposed to be causing trouble. I asked questions when Randy and Keith were in front of the court, too. I was only trying to be fair both times. Randy and Keith admitted they were guilty. There wasn't anything anyone could do."

"Did you really talk the court into letting Tony off?" asked Jana.

Katie sighed. "All I said was, since the bell hadn't rung and there were kids still not in their seats, it didn't seem fair to accuse him of disrupting class. That's all. Besides," Katie added, glaring in Laura's direction, "what goes on in Teen Court is *supposed* to be confidential."

"Do you really like Tony Calcaterra?" asked Melanie.

"That has nothing to do with it. I mean, no. He's just a show-off. You know how I feel about boys like that." She looked at her friends pleadingly.

Just then the first bell sounded for classes. "Whew. Saved by the bell," said Christie. "Come on, let's talk about it later."

Katie felt blue all morning. Everything her teachers said seemed to be coming through a fog. So far, being a judge in the Teen Court was a disaster.

Laura McCall was making up stories about Katie's letting Tony Calcaterra off because she liked him, and Beth and Jana were mad at her. Why didn't they understand that she was just trying to be fair? She didn't even like Tony. In fact she might even hate him. So what if he was cute? All he could do was stand around and flex his muscles. Still, she couldn't help admiring the way he stood up for himself. He was definitely independent, and she usually liked that in a person. But in Tony? she wondered. In macho, show-off Tony? She probably should have kept her mouth shut and not asked Mr. Naset all those questions. Especially since he was probably the one blabbing the courtroom proceedings all over school.

"I should have let him be convicted," she said to herself in the middle of Family Living class. "I should have recommended hanging."

Mary Sweeney, who was sitting in the next row, looked at Katie as if she thought she were talking to her. Katie smiled and shook her head.

At lunchtime, when Katie joined her friends at the group's favorite table, Beth and Jana were eating their lunches quietly while Melanie and Christie chattered away. Katie knew Beth and Jana were still angry over Randy and Keith's punishment, but she didn't know what she could do about it. In the meantime Christie and Melanie were obviously trying to heal the rift between their friends.

"How is the yearbook coming?" Melanie asked Jana.

Her response was a brief "Fine."

Christie raised her eyebrows in sympathy with Melanie's effort to get Jana to talk. She broke her sandwich in half and made her own try at lifting the gloom that hung over their table by raising a subject that was dear to Beth's heart.

"Oh, by the way, I heard they've decided to get the Indian mascot costume we suggested in my platform for the elections. Isn't that great?"

Katie could see that, in spite of herself, Beth's ears perked up.

"How are they going to decide who will wear it?" Katie asked, trying to keep the momentum going. If they could get Beth talking, maybe they could draw in Jana, too.

Christie seemed to catch on to what Katie was trying to do because she said, "I think they'll have tryouts and pick several people who will trade off. Are you going to try, Beth?"

Beth turned her apple over and looked at it. It seemed as if she was trying hard to act indifferent.

"Probably."

Katie gave Christie a weak smile at the failed attempt and settled back to eat her lunch.

Suddenly there was a commotion near the door to the kitchen. Katie glanced around to see Keith Masterson and Randy Kirwan sweeping out through the swinging doors carrying sudsy sponges. They were wearing paper chef's hats and aprons and had drawn curving black mustaches on their upper lips with Magic Marker. *"Messieurs! Mesdemoiselles!"* they shouted in unison, thrusting their sponges into the air with such gusto that soapy water ran down their arms and soaked their shirtsleeves. "We are at your service."

Laughter erupted in the crowded cafeteria, and Katie could see that the two boys were having a hard time keeping straight faces themselves.

Spotting the table where The Fabulous Five sat, Randy cried, "Aha!" and raced toward them. "A SPECK!" he shouted, pouncing on an imaginary spot and scrubbing furiously.

By this time the entire cafeteria was up for grabs. Kids clapped and whistled and shouted as Randy and Keith ran from table to table calling out *"Voilà!"* as they washed away spills and splattered soap suds all over the laughing students.

Katie couldn't help looking out of the corner of her eye at Jana and Beth as their solemn expressions turned first to surprise, then to comprehension, and finally to the same kind of amusement as everyone else's.

When the boys finally disappeared back into the kitchen and the cafeteria returned to normal, Jana looked sheepishly at Katie and said, "Did you see that? They were having a ball. I guess it's a little silly to be mad at you for punishing Randy and Keith when they don't seem to mind at all."

"Yeah," admitted Beth. "We were definitely over-reacting. I wouldn't blame you if you were mad at us."

"Forget it," said Katie, reaching toward each of them and giving their hands a quick squeeze.

As relieved as she was that her friends weren't mad at her anymore, some things didn't get any better for Katie in the afternoon. Namely, the rumors about Tony Calcaterra. In English class Kim Baxter leaned over and said, "I hear you like Tony Calcaterra. Are you dating?"

"No!" Katie shot back angrily. "Where did you hear that?"

"Melissa McConnell was telling me that she heard you helped get him off when Mr. Naset took him to the Teen Court. She said that he walked you home later, too."

Katie was so angry that her red hair seemed to burn her scalp. "Melissa McConnell and her friends don't know what they're talking about. I do *not* like Tony Calcaterra. He's just a show-off, and I wouldn't date him if he were the last boy on earth."

Later that afternoon Katie had the same conversation with Gloria Drexler and Marcie Bee. She was so depressed that she decided to skip going to Bumpers after school.

As she was walking out of the building, she saw a crowd of shouting kids gathered in a circle on the sidewalk in front of the school.

Someone shouted, "Get him!"

Katie stood on her tiptoes to see what was going on inside the circle. Someone was fighting.

She pulled Mona Vaughn's arm. "Who is it?"

"Clarence Marshall and Tony Calcaterra. Clarence said something to Tony about his earring."

Katie rolled her eyes. Oh, no, she thought. Tony's just gotten out of one jam and now he's in another.

The door to the school slammed, and Mr. Bell came storming across the school ground.

"STOP IT! STOP IT IMMEDIATELY!" he shouted, making his way to the center of the circle.

He reached down and separated Tony and Clarence, pulling them to their feet. "STOP IT, YOU TWO!"

"He started it," growled Clarence, blood running from his nose.

Tony looked at him coldly and didn't say a word.

"I don't care whose fault it is. I want you both in my office RIGHT NOW!"

Tony dusted off his pant legs and looked boldly at the spectators. Then his eyes fell on Katie, and he smiled.

"See you in court," he said, laughing.

CHAPTER

*T*hat night Katie tossed and turned in bed, worrying about the long week ahead. It would be four whole days before Teen Court met again on Friday and heard the case against Clarence and Tony for fighting. Four days for Laura and her friends to spread rumors about a romance between her and Tony. Four days for people to question her about how she would vote or what kind of punishment she would go for.

She was feeling more depressed than she had felt in a long time when she left for school the next morning, and she had barely gotten there when her first nightmare came true.

"Well, if it isn't *Her Honor.*"

Katie spun around to see who had spoken. It had sounded like Laura McCall's voice, so she wasn't surprised to see The Fantastic Foursome standing in a group nearby.

"I'll bet she's already thinking about how to put the blame for Tony and Clarence's fight on Clarence so that she can get Tony off again," said Laura. She was looking at her friends as she spoke, but it was obvious that she meant for Katie to hear.

Katie's temper started building like a mushroom cloud. "Listen, Laura McCall, I'm tired of your mean gossip. There's nothing between Tony Calcaterra and me, and you know it."

"Oh, is that right?" Laura asked in a fake-sweet voice. Then turning to her friends, she added, "That's not what we hear. Is it?"

"Well, what you hear is wrong!" came an angry voice from behind Katie. This time the voice was a welcome one, and Jana stepped up beside Katie and glared at the startled Fantastic Foursome. "Katie can't stand Tony Calcaterra. He's nothing but a macho jerk! Maybe one of *you* ought to go out with him."

Laura raised her nose into the air and then wheeled around and led her friends away. After they had gone, Katie let out a sigh of relief and smiled at Jana.

"Thanks," she said.

Jana returned the smile. "The Fabulous Five sticks together. Right?"

"Right!" echoed Katie.

The entire school was talking about the fight the afternoon before, and in practically every class that day someone asked Katie how she planned to vote. By the next day, Wednesday, there was a rumor going around that some of the seventh-grade boys were even betting among themselves that Katie would try to influence the rest of the court to get Tony out of trouble.

"I'm going to resign from Teen Court," Katie declared in frustration as she and her friends sat in a booth in a back corner of Bumpers after school.

"Don't you dare do that," said Melanie. "You know it's Laura McCall who's behind all those rumors about you and Tony."

"And Tammy Lucero," added Christie. "She's the world's worst gossip. I saw her talking to Kim Baxter and Sara Sawyer in the girls' bathroom this afternoon. They all shut up when I walked in, so you can bet what they were talking about. You and Tony."

"It isn't fair," grumbled Katie. "Maybe I shouldn't have argued for Tony last week. Everybody knows he's a troublemaker. Even if he got punished for something he didn't do that time, it would probably only make up for a bunch of other times when he got away with things."

Jana shook her head. "I can't believe you're saying that, Katie Shannon. Not after all the times you've yelled about how everything should be fair."

Katie didn't answer. But for the next two days she thought about Jana's words. Jana had been right, of course. Katie knew she couldn't throw away all the things she believed in just because things were getting tough.

Taking a deep breath, she pushed open the glass doors to the media center on Friday afternoon and went in. Everyone else had gotten there ahead of her and had already arranged the tables and chairs.

"We should get out of here pretty early today, don't you think?" asked Whitney as Katie sat down next to her. "I mean, everybody knows they really were fighting. What's to decide except for the punishment?"

Katie shrugged. "Is that the only case we have?"

"I don't think so," said Whitney. "I heard yesterday that two eighth-grade girls got caught smoking out on the parking lot behind Mr. Neal's van." Whitney's eyes were twinkling with laughter. "They thought nobody would see them, but Mr. Bartosik noticed smoke rising over the top of the van and thought it was on fire. Isn't that a riot?"

Katie couldn't help but laugh. "Talk about dumb," she said, shaking her head.

By now Mrs. Brenner was calling for quiet. "All right, everyone," she said. "We'd better get started. The first case has to do with a fight on the school grounds between Clarence Marshall and Tony Calcaterra. Mr. Bell is the plaintiff. Now," she said, looking at her notes. "We need to choose the officers for today. Let's see. Garrett, will you be the bailiff? Daphne, you be the clerk, and . . ." She hesitated as she looked over her list of names. "Katie, please be the senior judge."

Katie rocked back in her chair and stared dumbfoundedly at Mrs. Brenner. She wanted Katie to be the judge in Tony Calcaterra's case. This could be the end of her life at Wacko Junior High.

CHAPTER

10

"But Mrs. Brenner," said Katie, trying to keep her voice from quavering. "Shouldn't we let a ninth- or eighth-grader be senior judge? This is only our second meeting."

Katie could see Kaci smirk and look up at the ceiling.

"No. I think you'll do just fine. Miss Dickinson thought you would be a good choice, and I agree." She handed Katie a sheet of paper with the information about the cases on it. Katie looked at Miss Dickinson in amazement.

"Garrett, would you get the plaintiff and defendants for the first case?" asked Mrs. Brenner.

Katie sank into her chair. How could this be happening to her? Could she even look Tony Calcaterra in the eyes without stuttering or saying something dumb? Would she really be too easy on him? Maybe she could say she suddenly felt sick and had to go home. She glanced at Mrs. Brenner for help, but instead she gave Katie an encouraging smile. Katie smiled back weakly and gripped her hands tightly in her lap as the door opened, and Garrett led Mr. Bell, Tony, and Clarence in.

They marched down the aisle with Mr. Bell in front, like a warden bringing two prisoners to trial. Clarence slouched behind him, a small bandage over one eye.

Tony brought up the rear. He stood so tall and looked so proud, with his head held high, that if she hadn't known better, Katie would have thought he was coming to accept an award. His black hair was combed neatly in contrast to Clarence's, and his dark eyes flashed around the room like lasers from a star wars movie. Katie felt the warm feeling creeping over her again. She gulped. She knew her face was turning red. He was handsome.

She shook her head to clear away the thought and arranged the paper and pencil neatly on the table in front of her, trying to look unconcerned while her insides churned.

She pretended to look interested in the paper as Mr. Bell and the two boys took the chairs in front of the court, and all the while she knew Tony was looking at her. Her eyes betrayed her and she looked up at him. It was as if she had been hit by an electric shock. He smiled ever so slightly.

Katie steeled herself and put her fingertips to her forehead, trying to concentrate on the charge against Tony and Clarence that was written on the paper.

Taking a deep breath, she said, "Would the clerk read the charge?"

"Mr. Bell has brought the complaint of fighting on the school grounds against Clarence Marshall and Tony Calcaterra," said Daphne.

"Is there anything further you would like to say, Mr. Bell?" Katie asked.

Mr. Bell smiled at her confidently. "No. The charge speaks for itself. It really doesn't make any difference who started the fight; fighting in the school or on the school grounds is prohibited.

"However, once the court has taken care of that charge, I have a related matter for your consideration. It shouldn't take much of your time."

Katie made a note: *Mr. Bell has something else to talk about.* She wondered what it was but hurried on.

"Clarence Marshall or Tony Calcaterra"—Katie stiffened as she said Tony's name—"do either of you have anything to say?"

"He started it," said Clarence huffily. "He shoved me."

She looked at Tony questioningly, expecting him to say something. Tony shrugged as if he didn't care what Clarence said.

"Tony," broke in Shelly Bramlett, "did you shove Clarence?"

"I suppose so."

"Why?"

"It seemed like a good thing to do."

"Come on, Tony," said Shane. "You didn't do it for no reason. Why did you do it?"

Katie was overjoyed. While the others were asking questions, she could stay out of the case. Tony would know she wasn't interested in him, and no one could accuse her of playing favorites, which was ridiculous because she wouldn't do that anyway.

"He said something I didn't like, that's all. It was my fault. I should have considered his mental condition and let it go."

Shane casually covered his mouth with his hand. Katie could see the corners of his eyes crinkle.

"What did you say to him, Clarence?" asked D. J.

Clarence wiggled in his seat. "Nothing much. I guess I shouldn't of said it, though." He looked at Tony.

"What was it?" pursued D. J.

Clarence looked uncomfortable as the court waited. Finally his answer gushed forth. "I just said he looked like a sissy with that earring in his ear." His face turned red and he looked down at the floor.

"I'm sorry I said it. It was kind of dumb." He peeked up at the court through his hair, which was in his eyes, as usual.

Katie looked first at Clarence and then at Tony. Clarence was in trouble a lot, but he wasn't mean. How in the world could he say such a thing to Tony? He should have known what would happen. Still, Tony could have walked away. That's the macho world of men for you, Katie thought. They were both equally at fault.

Tony sat quietly observing the proceedings as if they had nothing to do with him. His arms were folded in a relaxed way. He wasn't trying to show off his muscles, but they stood out in sharp relief under his shirt. His square jaw was chiseled below his dark hairline. The earring looked natural on him.

Katie was surprised at her thought. The earring didn't look strange. Not on Tony. It was a part of his character. Everybody wears T-shirts that tell something about themselves. Beth wore some strange outfits sometimes, but they were just a part of her personality. Even Laura McCall wore her hair in that long braid because it made a statement that she must like. The earring was just part of his charisma.

Now that Katie thought about it, it wouldn't seem right if Tony didn't wear the earring. It was just him.

What am I thinking? she wondered. He doesn't have charisma.

"Katie, I think we had better keep going." Mrs. Brenner's words startled her out of her thoughts.

"Oh . . . uh . . . yes," she fumbled, and then recaptured her composure.

"Do any of you have any more to say?" She directed the question at Mr. Bell and the boys.

"Does anyone on the court have any other questions?"

The court responded with shakes of their heads.

"Garrett, er, bailiff," said Katie, "would you take the plaintiff and the defendants into the other room while the court discusses the case? We'll call you back as soon as we've decided."

CHAPTER

11

*K*atie was pleased with the way the court decided the case. Except for things she had to say as senior judge, she managed to stay out of the discussion. This time no one could claim she wasn't fair, she thought smugly.

It had only taken five minutes for the court to decide that since they had caused a disturbance, Tony and Clarence should both be hall monitors for a week. They would have to check passes and stop people from running or doing anything that was against the rules. Since both Clarence and Tony had seemed sorry about the fight, everyone agreed that was punishment enough.

Katie tried to suppress the giddiness she felt. She had to admit that she was glad the punishment hadn't been worse. It was just that neither Clarence nor Tony had meant to fight, she told herself.

She was smiling happily when Garrett brought Mr. Bell and the boys back into the room.

"Clarence Marshall and Tony Calcaterra," she announced. "The Teen Court has decided that, since you are both guilty of breaking the rule about no fighting in the school or on the school grounds, you both are to be hall monitors for one week. You will report to the Administration Office on Monday morning before school to get your instructions."

Tony and Clarence started to get up to leave.

"Just one moment," said Mr. Bell. "Clarence, you may go, but Tony, I'd appreciate it if you stayed. There's one other thing that needs discussing."

When Clarence had left, Mr. Bell began: "I'm sorry to bring this up without forewarning the court, but I've discussed this with Tony, and he knew I was going to do it."

The judges sat forward attentively. Katie was confused. What could be so important?

"The issue is: boys wearing earrings in school. It's against the dress code, and Tony knows it. I've talked to him about it three or four times, but he says it's his right to wear it, and he doesn't intend to stop.

"In all fairness to the court, I must tell you that this has been an issue in other schools. Some schools have changed their dress codes to accept earrings on boys and some have not, but here at Wakeman it is definitely against the rules. As you know, I feel strongly about the Teen Court concept, and rather than shield it from difficult issues, I decided to bring it before you."

The kids on the court sat back, speechless.

Thoughts raced through Katie's mind like runaway mice. She had just been so relieved about not having to get too deeply involved in deciding about Tony's punishment for fighting with Clarence, and now she was thrown into a much bigger case involving him. The worst thing was, she liked his earring.

Perspiration broke out on her forehead. What was she going to do? The fair thing to do didn't seem at all clear this time.

Kids wear all kinds of things that are different, like T-shirts, she thought. No one says anything as long as they aren't obscene or don't have beer commercials on them. Boys wear necklaces, only they call them chains. What's the difference? Katie flushed. What was she going to do? She didn't have the slightest idea.

She pulled herself together and looked Tony directly in the eyes. "Tony, do you have anything to say?"

He sat up straight. For the first time his face was serious. "Yes. I don't think my wearing an earring bothers anyone. There's nothing obscene about it, it's just an earring. There are hundreds of them in Wakeman. Just because I wear one doesn't change that.

"I could understand why they wouldn't like it if I wore a dress." Several of the kids on the court smiled. "That would disturb people. I'm not about to do that. I just think the rule is wrong if it says guys can't wear earrings. Hey, we wear chains around our necks, and girls wear pants."

Katie made notes on what he said.

"Does anyone have any questions?" she asked.

Heads shook all around the table.

"May I say one more thing?" Tony asked politely.

"Yes," answered Katie. Then she prayed silently that what he was going to say would be something that would make the decision easier.

Tony looked at each court member in turn before he spoke. "There's a lot of talk these days about discrimination, especially discrimination against women." He paused and looked sheepishly at Katie. "The trouble is, discrimination can be a two-way street, and a lot of people don't think about that. That's all I wanted to say. Thanks for listening."

Katie's head was swirling. She barely heard Mrs. Brenner when she said, "Garrett, would you take Mr. Bell and the defendant out? We'll get back to you as soon as we can."

Katie couldn't look at the others. Not yet. She had too much to think about first. Tony was right about discrimination, even though he was the last person on the planet whom she would have expected to feel that way. And yet, she had never thought about discrimination applying to boys as well as girls. Maybe he was right about that, too. Maybe, if you got right down to it, they both felt the same way about what was really fair and what wasn't. It might explain why they seemed to be attracted to each other.

"I think we'd better get started discussing this," Mrs. Brenner said, interrupting her thoughts.

Katie nodded. What would she say? How would they feel if she suggested that they disagree with the policy about boys' wearing earrings? It was one thing to disagree with one teacher, such as Mr. Naset, who really was in the wrong, but what could they do about bucking a school policy? It was the law in school. Katie had never thought about going against a law. But this law wasn't fair.

Would they think she was doing it just because it was Tony? She had tried to tell them she didn't like Tony, but now she wasn't sure. Maybe she did like him, after all.

"Well, it looks as if we've got another one that's pretty cut and dried," said Kaci. "Tony knows he's breaking a rule, and he doesn't intend to stop."

"But what kind of punishment?" asked Whitney.

"It doesn't seem as if what he has done is all that bad," said Kyle, doodling on his pad of paper.

"Hey, you ought to see some of the earrings my dad wears," said Shane, laughing. "He's got some dangles you wouldn't believe, and one he wears during the Christmas season even lights up."

Katie couldn't help but smile. She knew that Shane's mom and dad had been hippies during the nineteen sixties and had never grown out of it. It was one of the reasons that he was so laid back.

"But a rule is a rule," said Kaci. "He can't just do whatever he wants."

Shelly Bramlett joined in. "I know, but it does seem as if it's not right."

"A rule is a rule, right?" said Kaci, looking at the two advisers.

"That's right," answered Miss Dickinson. "Congress makes the laws. The courts have to interpret and apply the laws."

A glimmer of hope lit a light in Katie's head. "What does the rule say exactly?" she asked.

Miss Dickinson looked at her as several of them opened their student handbooks.

"I've got it," said Whitney, quickly reading the section on the dress code. "The rule says that boys will not wear earrings."

The light went out.

Katie straightened her back and stuck out her chin. She could feel the roots of her red hair tingling.

"I think the rule is wrong and ought to be changed," she blurted out. "As Tony said, guys do wear necklaces now. Only they call them chains. They would have been laughed at for doing that not so long ago." She could hear her voice rising, but she couldn't stop. "It *is* discrimination."

Jumping to her feet, she rushed on, feeling the words tumble out in her excitement. "Have you seen some of the outfits that are worn around Wakeman? His earring is tame compared to some of them. It's not *fair* to penalize him for not following a rule that doesn't make sense!"

Everyone was turned toward her when she finished. Miss Dickinson's mouth was set in a hard line.

Now I've done it, thought Katie.

CHAPTER

12

"But it's a *rule*," said Kaci. "As Miss Dickinson said, a court doesn't make laws, it just interprets them."

"But it's not *fair*," said Katie. She knew she was getting in deeper and deeper, but she couldn't back down now. As Willie and Jana had said, you have to stand up for the things you believe in. This rule *wasn't* fair, and that was a fact.

Everyone at the table started jumping into the argument. Some of the kids sided with Katie, and others sided with Kaci. The room was filled with rising voices.

"Wait a minute! Wait a minute!" cried Mrs. Brenner, standing to be heard above the noise. "Everyone quiet down!"

When they had settled back in their seats, she straightened her jacket and cleared her voice. "Please. It's obvious, to say the least, that you all have strong opinions about the matter, but let's stay calm.

"Now. What we have on the one hand is a rule that says boys will not wear earrings in school. On the other hand we have Tony, who doesn't feel the rule is fair and has decided not to obey it. What are our options?

"It's also obvious that it's not possible to satisfy everyone. It seems to me that in order to be *fair*," she looked over her glasses at Katie as she said the word, "we can do one of two things."

Everyone was listening to her intently.

"As we have said, there is a policy that must be followed." She raised her hand as Katie started to protest. "If, however, some of you feel strongly enough about the rule, we can work to get it changed." She paused to let what she had said sink in.

"You can either decide to punish Tony under the rule or, perhaps, suspend the case and petition the administration to change the rule. If you do the latter, Tony would have to agree to stop wearing the earring until a decision is made."

The students stirred in their chairs.

"A good idea," said Garrett.

"I like it," said Shelly.

Others nodded in approval.

Katie liked the idea, too.

"There, of course, will have to be someone willing to be chairperson of the committee to develop the petition." Mrs. Brenner was looking directly at Katie when she said it.

Katie sank back in her seat and raised her hand slowly.

"I will," she said weakly. She was cornered. What else could she do?

"If that's what the majority wants," Mrs. Brenner stressed.

It was.

Katie felt as if she had just been dropped into a deep, dark well with walls of wet, slippery stones. There was no way she was going to be able to climb out.

She had tried to avoid taking sides and having it seem as if she were for Tony because she had a crush on him. But darn it, she argued to herself, the rule wasn't fair. She would feel the same way if it had been Clarence who was wearing the earring.

How was she going to explain that to her friends, though? Jana and Beth weren't mad at her anymore, but still, they might feel that they had been right in the first place and that she liked Tony and was playing favorites. She felt as if she were the one on trial as Garrett brought Mr. Bell and Tony back into the room.

Katie cleared her throat. "The court has mixed opinions about the rule that prohibits boys from wearing earrings."

Mr. Bell raised his eyebrows at her statement.

"Therefore, we have decided to suspend the case to allow time for a petition to be made to the administration to revise the rule. Tony, if you agree not to wear the earring while the rule change is being considered, the court won't rule on your punishment at this time. If the rule is changed, there will be no punishment. If it isn't, the court will decide then what the punishment will be." She took a deep breath and looked straight at Tony. "Do you agree not to wear the earring?"

Both Tony and Mr. Bell looked surprised.

Tony frowned and thought for a minute before he asked, "Who's going to petition the administration?"

Katie took a deep breath. "A committee of Shane Arrington, Kyle Zimmerman, and Daphne Alexandrou will do that." Then she said more softly than she wanted to, "I'm going to be chairperson."

Tony looked at her for what seemed like hours.

Fear rushed through Katie. Was he going to refuse? If he did, she would look like a fool. Everyone in Wakeman would be laughing at her. The thought hadn't crossed her mind that he might not agree to stop wearing the earring. She saw herself walking down the long halls with people on both sides talking and pointing at her. She knew her face must have gone pale. Her red hair had probably turned white.

Tony smiled at her and reached up and took the earring from his ear. He dropped it into his shirt pocket.

Relief rushed back into Katie. She thanked him with her eyes.

After Tony and Mr. Bell left, Garrett went to get the people for the next case.

Now that Tony's hearings were over, Katie breathed a sigh of relief. She hadn't expected to be appointed senior judge or chairperson of a committee to petition for a change in student rules, but she had gotten through it. Except for explaining what had happened to her friends, the worst had to be over. The next case couldn't be as bad as the last, and the next time the Teen Court met, someone else would be senior judge. And as far as she was concerned, they could *have* it.

She looked up just as Garrett entered the room. Mr. Bartosik, the head custodian, was following Bonnie Zaretki and Linda Compton, the two eighth-grade girls who were caught smoking behind Mr. Neal's van. Katie smiled as she noticed that the custodian had slicked down his graying hair and was wearing a very serious expression. The two girls, on the other hand, seemed to be taking great pains to show everyone how unconcerned they were by laughing and whispering together and tossing smug looks at the court.

Daphne read the complaint. "Mr. Bartosik has brought the complaint of smoking in the faculty parking lot against Bonnie Zaretki and Linda Compton."

Linda took a brush out of her purse and began brushing her long, dark hair while Bonnie patted her mouth in what Katie was certain was a fake yawn. What's wrong with those two? she wondered. Don't they realize how serious it is to be brought before Teen Court?

She frowned and turned to the custodian, who sat uneasily on the edge of his chair. "Mr. Bartosik, is there anything you would like to add?"

"No, ma'am. It's just like I told Mr. Bell. I looked out and saw little puffs of smoke rising over Mr. Neal's customized van, and I thought maybe it was on fire. Not a big fire, you understand. There weren't any flames, or anything. But it could have been a small fire smoldering in the upholstery. Anyway, when I went to investigate, I found these two smoking."

Just then the door to the media center burst open and a man and a woman charged in. The man wore a business suit and carried a briefcase that he slammed down on the end of the table where the defendants sat. At the same instant both Bonnie and Linda began to smile.

"I'm Carl Zaretki, and I'm an attorney and Bonnie Zaretki's father," the man thundered. "And I protest these charges against *my* daughter and her friend. I'll have you know that I'm influential in town, and this so-called *Teen Court* has no business sitting in judgment of *my* Bonnie."

He sneered in the direction of Katie and the other court members and went on, "I read the article in the newspaper Sunday, and I don't intend to let you get away with this. It's disgraceful when a school allows a mere janitor and a few students to 'get' someone as beautiful and popular as my daughter. A kangaroo court is all this is, set up by an inept school administration, and I won't have it. If you do anything but declare these girls innocent, I'll take all of you to a *real* court." He made a sweeping gesture to indicate that he was including students as well as faculty in his threat.

Katie's mouth dropped open. Now they've *really* done it to me, she thought.

CHAPTER

13

*W*as it still just Friday after school? Katie asked herself as she walked the final block to her house. It seemed as if a whole week had passed in one afternoon.

Mr. Bell had been called from his office to the media center. He had tried to calm Mr. Zaretki, saying that the school understood his feelings, but the Teen Court had been approved by the school board. He also said that since there was proof that Bonnie and her friend had broken a school regulation, the court intended to pursue it. All the time, Bonnie Zaretki and Linda Compton were watching what was happening with the lady who was obviously Mrs. Zaretki, and looking like a pair of cats who had just swallowed a very large canary.

Mr. Zaretki had started yelling about how his daughter wasn't going to be lynched by a bunch of juveniles, so Mr. Bell asked him to step down the hall to his office to continue the discussion. Mrs. Brenner had hurriedly called for a postponement of the case against the girls and declared the court session over for the day.

It was a scary time, and Katie was trembling when it was all over and she finally got away from the school and had time to think.

Not only that, she was exhausted. She should have known that things were going too well when they solved the fighting case so easily. Now all of a sudden she was heading a committee to try to change a school rule, Mr. Zaretki was probably going to take his daughter's case to court and she'd be a defendant, and everyone would think she had played favorites again.

On top of it all, the school probably wouldn't change the rule about boys' wearing earrings anyway, and Tony would be right back before the Teen Court. With her luck it would be her turn to be senior judge again when he came back, and it would be like being caught in a revolving door—going around in circles and never getting out. She could cry if it would do any good.

"Hi, babe. How are things going?" Willie asked as Katie came into the kitchen.

"Don't ask."

Willie dusted off the top of a can of tomato sauce and opened it. "Spaghetti tonight," she said brightly in an obvious attempt to be cheerful. Her face clouded when Katie didn't respond. "Bad day, huh?"

"Kind of rotten."

"Care to talk about it?" Willie pushed Libber off the counter where she had been watching a slow drip stretch out of the faucet and plop into the drain.

"I guess." Katie repeated her story for Willie, emphasizing the part about the petitions to change the school policy against earrings and how she was to be the chairperson.

"That does sound like a bad day, honey. What are you going to do?"

"Just what I'm doing, I guess," Katie answered. "I haven't done anything wrong, except maybe convince the entire student body of Wacko Junior High that I play favorites."

"Don't you think most kids will understand how fair you're trying to be if you talk to them?"

"Believe me, I've tried."

Willie was silent as she filled a pot with water and set it on the stove. As she took sticks of spaghetti out of a tall glass jar, she said, "You know, it sounds to me as if you hit it on the head, kiddo. Just keep doing what you're doing, and things will turn out okay."

"You make it sound so easy, Mom," said Katie.

Her mother looked up from stirring the spaghetti sauce and waved the wooden spoon at Katie. "You know, when I was in high school in the late sixties, we tried to change rules by protest and rebellion, and we often ended up alienating the very people who could make those changes. You kids are using the system to make changes, and I have a feeling it's going to be different for you."

"But it's so *hard*," protested Katie.

Her mom laughed and then winked. "Do you think our way was easy? We suffered for our principles. We—"

A grin broke out over Katie's face. "Okay, Mom. You're getting as melodramatic as Beth. Besides, I get the picture." Willie gave her a big hug. "I just think you should try to keep talking to the kids at school who don't understand. You might be surprised at how fast they'll come around."

All evening Katie thought over her mother's words. She thought about Tony, too. Maybe she had been misjudging him all this time. Maybe all that macho stuff was just a cover-up. Hadn't he stood up for her when Clarence Marshall and Richie Corrierro were picking on her about her detention? And what about the trouble with Mr. Naset? Maybe he didn't stand up and fight for his rights then because Mr. Naset was discriminating against him for being in trouble so many other times, and he didn't think he could win.

Perhaps that was the real reason he always acted as if being in trouble was no big deal.

But now he was in trouble for something he cared a lot about, and he had decided to take a stand. She had to admire him for that, and she had to be true to herself and stand with him.

CHAPTER

14

*W*hen Katie got to the media center right after lunch on Monday for the meeting of the committee to work on changing the dress code, Shane, Kyle, and Daphne were already there. They were talking quietly among themselves.

"Have you heard anything more about what Mr. Zaretki is going to do?" Daphne asked her before she even sat down.

Katie shook her head. "I've tried not to think about it," she confessed. "I mean, it's one thing to be a judge or on the jury, but I don't even want to consider being a defendant in a *real* court."

"Us, either," said Kyle.

Katie could see that everybody was as upset as she was over Mr. Zaretki's threat. At this rate they wouldn't get any work done on the petitions unless she got them started.

"Okay, everybody," she said as she opened her notebook to a clean sheet of paper. "Why don't we write what we want to say first and then type it? After that we can make copies for the signatures."

"I'll type it," volunteered Daphne, her face brightening.

"I'll make the copies," said Kyle.

"What should we say in the application?" asked Katie.

"I think we ought to say it's a dumb rule," answered Shane.

"You can't do that," argued Daphne. "They won't even listen to you if you say it that way."

Katie nodded, thinking about what her mother had said about protest and rebellion in the sixties. "She's right. We've got to use diplomacy. Why don't we list all the reasons we think the rule ought to be changed first? And then we can decide what to say."

"Earrings are just jewelry like rings and necklaces," said Daphne. "There's no rule against boys' wearing rings and necklaces, and there shouldn't be one against wearing earrings."

"As long as they're regular earrings and there's nothing obscene or obnoxious about them," added Kyle.

"A lot of famous men wear them," added Shane. "You see them on TV all the time."

"Does that include your dad?" asked Daphne. Shane shoved her playfully.

Katie wrote as fast as she could. She added one of her own. "It's not fair to let girls wear them and not boys." Then, looking up, she asked, "Anything else?"

"It's a matter of self-expression," said Daphne.

"It's just plain dumb," said Shane, laughing. Daphne frowned at him.

"Why don't you guys try to think of more reasons while I write the beginning." Katie tore out the sheet and slid it across the table.

After they had worked in silence for a few minutes, she asked, "How does this sound?"

> *We, the undersigned students, do respectfully petition the administration of Wakeman Junior High to revise the Student Handbook to eliminate the rule against boys' wearing earrings in school for the following reasons:*

"I think we ought to add something that says they can't be wild," suggested Daphne.

Katie scribbled some more.

When they had finally agreed on the wording, Daphne typed it on one of the media center typewriters, and Kyle went to the copier and made half a dozen copies for each of them.

"If you let anyone take a petition to help you get signatures, keep track of who has it," Katie said. "And don't let anybody write funny stuff on them. You know, like Donald Duck . . . or worse."

Shane added, "Why don't we meet tomorrow at the same time and see how many signatures we have? Maybe we can turn them in then."

Katie signed her name to the first of her petitions in big bold letters and then stood at the door to her afternoon English class asking people to sign them. To her surprise not everyone did.

"Get real," said Shawnie Pendergast, a bouncy seventh-grader who had gone to Copper Beach Elementary. "Guys are guys. They don't need to wear earrings."

Even Alexis Duvall surprised Katie by refusing.

"Sorry," she said. "But the next thing you know they'll be wanting to wear miniskirts and panty hose. I just don't think it's masculine."

To Katie's relief most kids were willing to sign the petitions, including Joel Murphy, who grabbed the ballpoint pen out of Katie's hand, declaring that he would sign anything that would help change a school rule, no matter what it was. She had filled the first sheet and was waiting at the door to her last class of the day when Laura and Melissa McConnell came by.

"I hear you're trying to help your boyfriend out of trouble again," Laura said in a sickly sweet voice. "It would be nice if you tried half as hard for your friends."

The back of Katie's neck felt prickly. "It would be nice if you minded your own business."

"Oh, I want to help, too," Laura insisted. "Shane asked me if I would sign his petition, but when he said you were collecting signatures, I said I wanted to sign *yours*. I'd do *anything* to help a friend." Her voice dripped with sugar. "Wouldn't you?"

Grudgingly Katie handed Laura the paper and the pen. A signature was a signature, no matter what kind of snake signed it.

CHAPTER

15

The next morning, as Katie approached the school grounds, she saw Tony waiting by the gate. He pushed away from the post he was leaning against as she got near. Katie cringed inside when she saw the tiny gold earring in his ear. He was wearing it again.

"Hi," he said. "I owe you a second thanks, I guess. You're getting to be a real Sheena coming to my rescue all the time."

"I didn't come to your rescue," she said angrily. "And I see you've decided to flaunt that earring again. Couldn't you just wait until the committee had finished with the petition?"

"Oops!" he said with what seemed to be honest surprise.

"I meant to take this thing out before I got to school. Thanks for mentioning it." He removed it from his ear and dropped it into his pocket.

"There's no rule that says I can't wear it when I'm not at school. That reminds me, how's the big petition drive coming?"

"We've got a lot of signatures," Katie answered proudly. "We're going to count them after lunch."

"Did you get any flack about its not being masculine for guys to wear earrings?"

"Some," she admitted. "But not much. It's not that unusual to see guys wearing them nowadays. That's another reason I think these petitions are important."

Tony smiled. "I don't suppose it would help if I signed one of them? I could even get some guys to sign."

She looked closely at him. He seemed serious for a change. She wanted to believe that her new theory about him had been right. That being macho was mostly a cover-up. But she wasn't sure. Maybe she should test him.

"I thought your way was to go ahead and do what you wanted to without worrying about the rules," she challenged.

He chuckled. "It usually is. But since you're trying so hard to change the rule for me, I thought I ought to cool it," he answered smoothly. *Too* smoothly, thought Katie.

She shifted her books from one arm to the other to hide the disappointment she was sure was in her eyes. "I want you to understand, I'm *not* doing this for you. Just as I didn't argue to get you off when Mr. Naset complained about your disturbing class, just because it was you. The only reason I'm doing any of these things is because I want to be fair. You just *happened* to be there at the time."

He looked at her appraisingly. She didn't like his cool attitude. She had been wrong to think he was taking a stand for something he believed in. He was just putting on a show. If he thought he could get her to fall for him that way, he was dead wrong!

"Is that so?" he said with a smirk. "By the way, are you going out with anyone now?"

She could feel her face redden. "I never said I didn't go out."

"Maybe you and I could try it sometime."

"I, I . . ." She looked around for a way out. She saw her friends waiting by the fence and wanted to go over to them. He took her arm and stopped her.

"You're too busy fighting crime, huh? Are you going to be a lady lawyer or a judge?"

"Maybe a lawyer, and don't say *lady* lawyer. That's sexist," she said, sticking out her chin. "Anyway, I've thought about it."

"And maybe I'll get you to defend me then, too," he said with a sideways grin. "But I have to admit that I like you better as a judge. I can see the sign on your office window now. It says, 'Katie Shannon, Hanging Judge.'" He burst out laughing.

"I've got to go. My friends are waiting for me." She pulled her arm loose and darted toward the rest of The Fabulous Five.

"See you around, *Your Honor*," he called after her.

Katie met with the petition committee again after lunch.

"I filled up all my pages," said Daphne.

"Me, too," said Kyle. "It was pretty easy."

"Here are mine," said Shane.

Katie looked closely at his petitions and smiled. "Igor's name isn't on here, is it?"

Shane threw back his head and laughed at the mention of his pet iguana. "No. But it's only because he's mad that he doesn't have any ears to wear earrings in."

Daphne slugged him playfully.

"Let's count them," said Katie.

They had two hundred and twenty-eight signatures.

"That ought to convince Mr. Bell and the administration that the kids really think boys ought to be allowed to wear earrings," said Kyle.

"That doesn't mean they'll change the rule, though," said Daphne.

"Why not?" asked Katie.

"Well, there are a lot of things the kids might vote for that the school wouldn't allow."

"But Daph, this makes so much sense," Katie argued.

"To me, too. But we're not the ones running the school," Daphne said.

"I'm with you, Katie," agreed Shane. "I can't see how they can refuse."

"What will Tony do if it doesn't pass?" asked Kyle.

"More than likely get into trouble over it again," said Shane. "Nothing has changed to make him act differently, has it?"

"No, I guess not," Kyle replied.

Katie had to agree with them.

The four of them marched to the office together with their stack of petitions.

"May I help you?" asked Miss Simone, the office secretary.

Katie stepped forward and laid the pile of petitions on her desk.

"We'd like to file this petition for a change in the dress code in the student rule book." she said proudly.

"My, you have a lot of signatures here."

"Two hundred and twenty-eight," Katie said, grinning at the others.

"Well, I'll give this to Mr. Bell right away. He has a staff meeting on Friday morning, and I'm sure he'll bring it up then."

Katie looked at the others and held up crossed fingers for good luck. The decision on the dress code rule would probably be made by the next session of Teen Court.

CHAPTER

*F*riday morning Katie was so nervous she felt like a balloon that wanted to take off and zip around the sky. This morning Mr. Bell and his staff were going to decide whether or not to go along with the petition. If they decided against it, what would Tony do? If they didn't change the rule and he wouldn't quit wearing the earring, he might even be suspended from school. That would mean he would have to come before the Teen Court again this afternoon. He might even think that Katie hadn't tried hard enough to get the rule changed.

She shook her head. It's silly to worry about that. He doesn't like me. I'm just another girl for him to flex his muscles at and dazzle with his smile.

The morning dragged on for what felt like a month. Her mind kept wandering to Mr. Bell's staff meeting.

They ought to be meeting now, she thought. Who would be arguing to change the rule? Would Mr. Bell be for it or against it?

The meeting must be over now, she thought later. She had looked at her watch every two minutes all morning. What had they decided? Katie had a feeling of finality. It had to be finished. Whatever the decision was, it had been made, and it might affect her life forever.

At lunch Jana, Beth, Christie, and Melanie all tried to be cheerful, but Katie knew they were watching her out of the corners of their eyes.

Finally Jana spoke. "No matter what happens with the petitions, Katie, you really did a great thing. Not very many kids would have had the nerve to start a petition drive to legalize earrings at school."

"And we know that you did it because you believe it's fair," Christie assured her, "*not* because you were playing favorites with Tony Calcaterra."

"We're with you one hundred percent," said Melanie.

Katie's eyes got misty. Even though she knew they were behind her, hearing them say it was exactly what she needed at that moment. "One more time: The Fabulous Five stick together!" she said, raising her milk carton.

The five best friends tapped their milk cartons together.

"Right on!" said Beth.

The public address system interrupted their celebration.

"Will the members of the Teen Court please report to Mr. Bell's office?"

"Uh-oh," said Katie. "Wish me luck, gang. This is it."

She tried not to panic as she made her way to the office. The other eight members of the court crowded into the small room where the principal and Mrs. Brenner and Miss Dickinson were already waiting.

When everyone was inside, Mr. Bell rose from behind his desk, cleared his throat, and said, "I want to thank you for your attempt to change a rule that you felt was unfair in the same democratic way our country amends its laws. The staff members read your petition, noted the large number of signatures in support of it, and discussed it at great length. The vote was a close one"—he paused—"but I'm afraid it was against your petition. Earrings will not be permitted on males in Wakeman Junior High."

Katie sank back in her seat, the earlier feeling of being a sky-bound balloon slowly passing away as if all the air had just leaked out.

Tears blinded Katie's eyes so that she couldn't look at her fellow Teen Court members. After all their hard work, the teachers had voted against them.

"One more thing," said Mr. Bell as some of the students moved toward the door. "On the matter of Bonnie Zaretki and Linda Compton . . ."

Everyone froze in their tracks as Mr. Bell went on, "They will return to Teen Court this afternoon."

Katie did a double take. All around her kids were whispering.

Mr. Bell held up his hand, signaling that he wasn't finished talking. "I want you to know how pleased and proud I am of the way the Teen Court is conducting itself. Junior high is a time of transition between the childhood years of elementary school and the more adult years of high school. Many people opposed the formation of Teen Court on the grounds that you were too young for the responsibility. I am proud to say that you have all shown maturity and judgment in your handling of the cases that have come before you, and I look forward to working with you in the future."

Mr. Bell dismissed them after that, and Katie turned to leave, feeling very mixed up. The vote against the student petition had disappointed her a lot, and she was nervous about Tony's coming back to court again. What would he do this time? How would he behave? She was nervous, too, about Bonnie and Linda's scheduled reappearance. Was Mr. Zaretki's threat over? Or was this just round two of the battle?

Still, Mr. Bell's praise of the court's maturity and judgment were important. He was right about the difference between elementary school and junior high. There was more trust and more concern with students' opinions here, and there was definitely more responsibility. No matter how much pressure it had put on her, she could never stop trying to be fair.

She sighed as she moved on toward the door, but Miss Dickinson caught her eye and motioned her to one side.

"Would you come to my room for a moment?" asked the teacher. "I'd like to talk to you."

Katie nodded, but she had an ominous feeling. Teachers didn't usually want to have talks unless your grades were bad or you had done something wrong.

"Pull up a chair," said Miss Dickinson when they reached her room. She almost sounded friendly, thought Katie. "I know, Katie, that you have a strong sense of fairness, and I think it's great. I've thought back about the time that I gave you a detention, and now I think maybe I was a little hasty. Maybe *I* wasn't as fair as I could have been. I'm sorry if that's true."

It took Katie a moment to answer. Miss Dickinson was apologizing to her. A teacher was actually admitting she was wrong.

"That's all right, Miss Dickinson."

"There's one more thing I wanted to talk to you about. Mrs. Brenner and I sat in on Mr. Bell's staff

meeting this morning when they considered your petition. I can't tell you who voted for or against it, but
there was a great deal of discussion and the vote was
very close.

"Now I don't want you to feel bad." She put her
hand on Katie's arm and her eyebrows pinched together. "What you did was a good thing, and you kids
tried very hard. What I wanted to say to you is, I think
that maybe if you try again in a few months, after Mrs.
Brenner and I have had a chance to do a little politick-
ing," she said, winking, "the petition might have a better chance of passing."

Katie's spirits soared and then fell. "What about
Tony?"

"I was hoping you might talk to him. If he starts
wearing the earring again, Mr. Bell will have no choice
but to bring him before the Teen Court again. It's the
rule. It may not seem fair, but Tony can't decide which
rules he likes and which ones he doesn't like." Then
she smiled and added, "I know you'll help him do
what's right."

Katie nodded. She got up to leave and then stopped.
"Miss Dickinson, thanks for what you said about my
detention. I think you're fair."

"Thank you, Katie."

For a second, Katie thought she saw tears in Miss
Dickinson's eyes.

"And Katie?"

"Yes, Miss Dickinson."

"Do talk to Tony. He'll listen to you."

Katie nodded and left the room. Miss Dickinson was right. Someone did need to talk to Tony. But why did it have to be her?

CHAPTER

17

Katie wasn't sure if she found Tony or he found her. He was standing in the hallway near her locker when she went to put away her things and get the books she needed for homework before she went to Teen Court.

"Hi," he said, flashing his insolent grin at her.

"Hi." She fumbled around, trying to find a way to begin telling him about the decision. She didn't feel hostile toward him at this moment.

She took a deep breath and said it. "Mr. Bell told the court that the petition didn't pass." She watched his face for any reaction. When there was none, she said quickly, "But Miss Dickinson told me that if we tried again in a few months, she thought it would. Could you wait until then before you started wearing the ear-ring again?" She looked at him hopefully.

He studied her face. "I've already decided not to wear it in school." He paused. "You'd look kind of bad if I did, wouldn't you? Like maybe you'd been taken in by me."

The question caught Katie by surprise. "That's not why I asked if you could wait," she said, frowning. "I think it's kind of dumb to get into trouble if there's a good chance the rule's going to be changed. I think Mr. Bell, Mrs. Brenner, and Miss Dickinson *are* trying to be fair. It just may take a little longer."

Tony smiled at her. This time he looked a little more sincere.

"Still trying to be a lawyer, aren't you?" he asked. "I already decided not to wear it at school if the petition didn't pass. I don't want people thinking I sat back and watched while you did all the work. I'm not the kind of guy who uses his friends."

She had never heard his voice so soft. And he had called her his friend. Did he mean it? His sparkling black eyes made her insides do somersaults.

"Now that I've said that, I've got another favor to ask," he said, grinning impishly. "When it comes time to petition again, will you help?"

Katie was flabbergasted. She looked at him help-lessly as she struggled for words. First he said he wouldn't use his friends, and then he asked for help again. What kind of guy was he, anyway?

Unruffled by her silence, Tony went on, "I was thinking that if the Wacko administration turns down the petition again, we could take it to the school board. And if they turn it down . . . who knows? With your help, we could take it all the way to the Supreme Court? What do you say, Your Honor?"

Katie was still confused. "But why me?"

"Because everybody knows you're fair and that you stand up for what you believe in. They wouldn't listen to me, but they would listen to you. Besides," he added with a sly smile, "I like red hair. You doing anything after school?"

Katie felt dizzy. One minute he was saying the things she wanted to hear—that he admired her for the qualities she was most proud of. But then, the next minute, he was behaving like his old macho self.

"I told my friends I'd meet them at Bumpers and then go to a movie with them," she said hurriedly before she could change her mind.

"Still not dating, huh?"

"Oh, no! I definitely date."

"Good. I'll remember that." He laughed and then added, "See you in court, Your Honor."

Katie watched as he walked away. It was crazy. She definitely didn't think he was her type. But what type was he? She still couldn't be sure. Maybe the best way to find out was to go on a date with him sometime, she mused. It would be the *fair* thing to do, she thought, smiling to herself.

Everyone was chattering happily as the Teen Court members settled into their chairs. Katie thought how close they all were becoming. They were developing friendships from having to do so much together and take so much responsibility.

She was really starting to enjoy Teen Court, especially now that her first turn at being senior judge was over and she had survived in one piece. It was even nice to know that Miss Dickinson had learned a lesson. Well, teachers were people, too, she guessed, chuckling quietly to herself.

This is what being in court is all about, and I like it. She stuck her chin out. Maybe she would be a lawyer someday, and maybe even a judge. *Her Honor, Katie Shannon* didn't sound too bad. She would have to try saying it out loud in the bathroom at home.

"Okay, everyone. Time to get the court in session," announced Mrs. Brenner.

"What about Tony Calcaterra?" asked Daphne.

Miss Dickinson looked at Katie. The others followed her lead.

"I talked to Tony," said Katie. "He says he isn't going to wear his earring at school until the rule is changed"—her voice dropped to just above a whisper—"and he asked if I'd help on the next petition."

"Katie and I discussed trying another petition at a later date," interjected Miss Dickinson. "Things do change. And Mr. Bell has agreed that Tony doesn't need to be punished this time, providing he really doesn't wear his earring to school again.

"All right!" said Shane.

"Well, we might as well get started," said Mrs. Brenner. "Daphne, why don't you be senior judge; Shane, you be bailiff; and Shelly, you can be clerk."

"Mr. Bailiff," said Daphne in a fake baritone voice. "Would you bring in the first plaintiff and defendant?"

"DE-lighted, Your Honor," said Shane.

There was a commotion at the back of the room as Shane led Bonnie Zaretki and Linda Compton into the media center. Right behind them was Mr. Bartosik, his hair slicked down again, and Mr. Bell. And behind them came Mr. and Mrs. Zaretki, looking angrier than ever.

"Oh, no," groaned Katie.

With loud scraping noises chairs were dragged across the floor so that Bonnie's parents could sit beside her. Mr. Bell stood to one side, his expressionless face giving away no clues as to what was to come.

All of the judges looked upset at the sight of the Zaretkis, but Shelly finally found her voice and repeated the charges from the week before.

"Do either of you have anything to say?" she asked the two girls.

Bonnie stood and smiled slyly at the court. "My father has decided not to take the Teen Court to *real* court," she began, looking over her shoulder at her father as if for reassurance. He nodded sternly, and she went on, "However, Linda and I have decided to circulate petitions to allow students to smoke on the school grounds."

Mrs. Brenner gasped, and several jurors dropped their pencils. Mr. Zaretki smiled pompously.

"It is our belief," said Bonnie, sounding to Katie as if she were reciting lines she had memorized, "that Linda Compton and I are being unfairly discriminated against by not being allowed to smoke and that—"

"Just a moment, here," said Mr. Bell in his sternest voice. He folded his arms across his chest and walked slowly to the end of the table where the members of the court sat. "We allowed the earring petition to be presented because it is proper to question the dress code from time to time."

Mr. Bell paused and looked directly at Mr. Zaretki. "But in the case of a petition to allow smoking, I want it understood right now that the administration will never, under any circumstances, permit anything that will be detrimental to our students' health or well-being. I want it further understood that petitioning the administration is not the solution to every question, nor will I allow this Teen Court to be intimidated. Now, *Mr. and Mrs. Zaretki*, Mr. Bartosik, and girls, if you will allow me, please. I think it's time for the court to make its decision."

When the room had been cleared, no one said a word. Katie stared at her notepad, thinking that it was so quiet you could almost hear the dust settle. She liked the way Mr. Bell had handled the problem, and she was sure that Mr. Zaretki would never interfere with school policy again.

Finally Shane spoke up. "There's no question that they're guilty, but I feel sorry for them. Bonnie's dad was the real villain."

"I agree," said Katie. Most of the others nodded.

After a few minutes discussion the court decided to sentence Bonnie and Linda to two weeks shelving books in the media center. When they heard the decision, the girls looked relieved.

"Can we leave now?" asked Katie after the girls were gone. She was exhausted and wanted to go home.

"Not yet," said Mrs. Brenner. "Shane, will you bring in our last defendant of the day, please?"

At the sound of the doors opening again, Katie looked up to see who was being brought in. Her mouth dropped open, and she fell back in her chair in total shock. *It was Mr. Bell and Tony.*

As they took their seats in front of the court, Katie looked frantically at Tony's ear. There was no earring.

Had he taken it out after Mr. Bell caught him wearing it at school? She narrowed her eyes and looked at him angrily. How could he have done such a thing? He had said he wouldn't. Couldn't he keep his word for one single day?

Shelly cleared her voice. "The charge of painting graffiti on the outside school wall has been brought against Tony Calcaterra by Mr. Bell."

Daphne asked, "Mr. Bell, is there anything you want to say?"

Mr. Bell sighed and looked at Tony, who sat gazing at Katie with that arrogant smile on his face. "The charge speaks for itself. Tony used a can of spray paint and sprayed letters on the outer wall of the school."

"What were the letters?" asked Shane.

"T. C. + K. S.," answered Mr. Bell.

Katie's mouth dropped open as everyone in the room looked her way.

Katie lounged on one end of the couch stroking Libber, who was gently kneading her stomach. Willie was seated at the other end reading and marking a manuscript. It had been an exciting and very confusing day, and Katie was definitely glad it was over.

When Mr. Bell had told them what Tony had done this time, she thought she would die right there in her chair. Everyone in the room knew what the letters meant. Tony Calcaterra + Katie Shannon. At the same time it kind of made her happy. Maybe Tony *really* did like her.

Kaci Davis had smirked her usual superior way when Katie said she thought she should abstain from voting on Tony's punishment. The Teen Court had decided that Tony should clean the letters off the wall along with some other graffiti that had been there before. That seemed fair. Even Tony had thought so, and he had winked at her as he left the room. She would have to give some serious thought to going out with him. Only to find out if he was on the level, of course, she assured herself.

She certainly had learned a lot about how tough being fair was in the last few days, and she would never *ever* again say the hard part was over. Each time she had, she had gotten hit with a bomb. First, her friends thought she was being too tough on Randy and Keith, and then practically everyone in Wacko Junior High thought she was being too easy on Tony.

It seemed as if adults didn't always know how to be fair either. She would never forget Mr. Zaretki, and Miss Dickinson had been unfair to Katie by giving her that detention. But she had apologized, and that was just about all you could do when you goofed.

Getting up, Katie carried Libber to her room and put her on the bed. Reaching into her closet, she pulled out her navy-blue blazer and put it on. Then she took an old briefcase of her mother's and posed in front of her full-length mirror.

Not bad, she thought. Maybe it's a little too early to think about becoming a judge, but I'm going to make a terrific lawyer.

CHAPTER

*B*eth was running late. Mr. Naset had sprung a pop quiz during history class, and she had put off doing her homework last night so that she could watch a movie on television. She had still been working on the quiz when the dismissal bell rang.

Now as she hurried into the dressing room of the girls' gym to change into shorts and sneakers for cheerleading practice, she crossed her fingers that Miss Wolfe hadn't already lined up the squad on the floor and started the warm-up stretching exercises. Miss Wolfe went positively berserk when anyone came in late.

"I'm in luck," she sang to herself as she saw that Alexis Duvall was sitting on a bench tying her shoes and Taffy Sinclair was still primping at the mirror. If she hurried, she would get onto the gym floor on time.

Beth was rushing so that she didn't notice when Alexis and Taffy left for the gym, and she was pulling on her shoes when she heard the sound of voices coming from the other section of the dressing room. It was the section where the restrooms and shower stalls were.

"That's not all my father lets me do."

The voice from behind the wall was faint, but there was no mistaking who was speaking. Beth narrowed her eyes and made a face. It was Laura McCall, and it sounded as if she was bragging again.

"I never have to be home at a certain time. I've never had a curfew in my life, and I don't even have to tell Dad where I'm going. You see, he trusts me totally."

"Must be nice!" answered someone Beth thought sounded like Dekeisha Adams. "My parents treat me like some kind of criminal. They check up on me and make me call if I'm going to be *one second* late. Then they give me the third degree when I get home. I'd give anything to have a father like yours."

Beth wanted to throw up. Laura was always trying to make people think that she was the luckiest person alive and that her good fortune would rub off on anyone who hung around her. Now she was trying to impress Dekeisha. It was disgusting.

Beth quickly tied her sneakers and started to gather up her things when Laura and Dekeisha came around the corner from the other section. The moment they spotted Beth, Laura whispered something to Dekeisha and both of them burst out laughing.

"I really feel sorry for *some* girls," said Laura between laughs. "Don't you, Dekeisha?"

The tall black seventh-grader looked sympathetically at Beth for an instant and then nodded as they raced out of the dressing room still laughing.

Beth felt rage creeping up her body and into her face like mercury rising in a thermometer. How dare Laura McCall make fun of me! She thought. I'd rather die than have anyone think I need sympathy. She may think she can make herself look great by making me look bad, but she's mistaken. I'll turn the tables on her if it's the last thing I ever do.

How will theatrical Beth deal with Laura's constant bragging? Will she put a stop to it once and for all? Or will her flair for being dramatic cause her to do things that will only make it worse and get herself into trouble? Find out in *The Fabulous Five #5: The Bragging War.*

ABOUT THE AUTHOR

Betsy Haynes, the daughter of a former newswoman, began scribbling poetry and short stories as soon as she learned to write. A serious writing career, however, had to wait until after her marriage and the arrival of her two children. But that early practice must have paid off, for within three months Mrs. Haynes had sold her first story. In addition to a number of magazine short stories and the Taffy Sinclair series, Mrs. Haynes is also the author of *The Great Mom Swap* and its sequel *The Great Boyfriend Trap*. She lives in Colleyville, Texas, with her husband, who is also an author.

GOOD NEWS! The five best friends who formed the AGAINST TAFFY SINCLAIR CLUB will be starring in a series all their own.

IT'S NEW. IT'S FUN. IT'S FABULOUS. IT'S THE FABULOUS FIVE!

From Betsy Haynes, the bestselling author of the Taffy Sinclair books, *The Great Mom Swap*, and *The Great Boyfriend Trap*, comes THE FABULOUS FIVE. Follow the adventures of Jana Morgan and the rest of THE FABULOUS FIVE as they begin the new school year in Wakeman Jr. High.

☐ SEVENTH-GRADE RUMORS (Book #1)

The Fabulous Five are filled with anticipation, wondering how they'll fit into their new class at Wakeman Junior High. According to rumors, there's a group of girls called The Fantastic Foursome, whose leader is even prettier than Taffy Sinclair. Will the girls be able to overcome their rivalry to realize that rumors aren't always true? 15625-X $2.75

☐ THE TROUBLE WITH FLIRTING (Book #2)

Melanie Edwards insists that she *isn't* boy crazy. She just can't resist trying out some new flirting tips from a teen magazine on three different boys—her boyfriend from her old school, a boy from her new school, and a very cute eighth-grader! 15633-0 $2.75/$3.25 in Canada

☐ THE POPULARITY TRAP (Book #3)

When Christie Winchell is nominated for class president to run against perfect Melissa McConnell from The Fantastic Foursome, she feels pressure from all sides. Will the sudden appearance of a mystery candidate make her a winner after all? 15634-9 $2.75

HER HONOR, KATIE SHANNON (Book #4)

When Katie Shannon joins Wakeman High's new student court, she faces the difficult job of judging both her friends and foes. On Sale: December 15640-3 $2.75

Watch for a brand new book each and every month!

Book #5 On Sale: January/Book #6 On Sale: February

Buy them at your local bookstore or use this page to order:

Great FREE offer
just for you!

Join SNEAK PEEKS™!

Do you want to know what's new before anyone else? Do you like to read great books about girls just like you? If you do, then you won't want to miss SNEAK PEEKS™! Be the first of your friends to know what's hot ... When you join SNEAK PEEKS™, we'll send you FREE inside information in the mail about the latest books ... *before they're published!* Plus updates on your favorite series, authors, and exciting new stories filled with friendship and fun ... adventure and mystery ... girlfriends and boyfriends.

It's easy to be a member of SNEAK PEEKS™. Just fill out the coupon below ... and get ready for fun! It's FREE! Don't delay—sign up today!

YOUR OWN

SWEET VALLEY HIGH

SLAM BOOK!

If you've read *Slambook Fever*, Sweet Valley High #48, you know that slam books are the rage at Sweet Valley High. Now *you* can have a slam book of your own! Make up your own categories, such as "Biggest Jock" or "Best Looking," and have your friends fill in the rest! There's a four-page calendar, horoscopes and questions most asked by Sweet Valley readers with answers from Elizabeth and Jessica

It's a must for SWEET VALLEY fans!

☐ 05496- FRANCINE PASCAL'S SWEET VALLEY HIGH
          SLAM BOOK
          Laurie Pascal Wenk $3.95

- -

Bantam Books, Dept. SVS5, 414 East Golf Road, Des Plaines, IL 60016

Please send me the books I have checked above. I am enclosing $_____
(please add $2.00 to cover postage and handling). Send check or money order—no cash or C.O.D.s please.

Mr/Ms _____

Address _____

City/State _____ Zip _____

SVS5—1/89

Please allow four to six weeks for delivery. This offer expires 7/89.

Skylark is Riding High with Books for Girls Who Love Horses!

☐ **A HORSE OF HER OWN by Joanna Campbell**
15564-4 $2.75
Like many 13-year-olds, Penny Rodgers has always longed to ride a horse. Since her parents won't pay for lessons, Penny decides to try her hand at training an old horse named Bones. When she turns him into a champion jumper, Penny proves to everyone that she's serious about riding!

☐ **RIDING HOME by Pamela Dryden**
15591-1 $2.50
Betsy Lawrence has loved horses all her life, and until her father's remarriage, was going to get her own horse! But now there's just not enough money. And Betsy can't help resenting her new stepsister Ferris, who is pretty, neat, does well in school, and gets all the music lessons she wants—Ferris loves music the way Betsy loves horses. Can the two girls ever learn to be sisters—and even friends?

New Series!

☐ **HORSE CRAZY: THE SADDLE CLUB: BOOK #1 by Bonnie Bryant**
15594-6 $2.95 Coming in September
Beginning with HORSE CRAZY: BOOK #1, this 10-book miniseries tells the stories of three very different girls with one thing in common: horses! Fun-loving Stevie and serious Carole are at Pine Hollow Stables for their usual lesson, when they meet another 12-year-old named Lisa. Her elaborate riding outfit prompts the girls to play a practical joke on her. After Lisa retaliates a truce is formed, and so is THE SADDLE CLUB!
Look for HORSE SHY: BOOK #2, Coming in October!
